Paul Leicester Ford

**The New England Primer**

a reprint of the earliest known edition - with many facsimiles and reproductions -

and an historical introduction

Paul Leicester Ford

**The New England Primer**
*a reprint of the earliest known edition - with many facsimiles and reproductions - and an
historical introduction*

ISBN/EAN: 9783337251130

Printed in Europe, USA, Canada, Australia, Japan

Cover: Foto ©Andreas Hilbeck / pixelio.de

More available books at **www.hansebooks.com**

*The*

# NEW-ENGLAND PRIMER

A REPRINT OF THE EARLIEST KNOWN
EDITION, WITH MANY FACSIMILES
AND REPRODUCTIONS, AND
AN HISTORICAL IN-
TRODUCTION

*Edited by* PAUL LEICESTER FORD

*NEW YORK*
Dodd, Mead and Company
M dccc xc ix

THE UNIVERSITY PRESS

DEDICATED

TO

*Mr. Cornelius Vanderbilt*

IN GRATEFUL

RECOGNITION OF COURTESIES

TO THE EDITOR

IN THE USE OF HIS

*Collection*

OF

NEW ENGLAND PRIMERS

Portrait of George Washington

(From the "New England Primer." Boston: [1-89?])

# INTRODUCTION

IN the apocryphal poem of John Rogers " unto his children," which was included in every New England Primer, he said :

> *" I leave you here a little booke*
> *For you to looke vpon,*
> *That you may see your father's face*
> *When I am dead and gon."*

No better description of the New England Primer itself could be penned. As one glances over what may truly be entitled " The Little Bible of New England," and reads its stern lessons, the Puritan mood is caught with absolute faithfulness. Here was no easy

1

road to knowledge and to salvation; but with prose as bare of beauty as the whitewash of their churches, with poetry as rough and stern as their storm-torn coast, with pictures as crude and unfinished as their own glacial-smoothed boulders, between stiff oak covers, which symbolized the contents, the children were tutored, until, from being unregenerate, and as Jonathan Edwards said, "young vipers, and infinitely more hateful than vipers" to God, they attained that happy state when, as expressed by Judge Sewall's child, they were afraid they "should goe to hell," and were "stirred up dreadfully to seek God." No earthly or heavenly rewards were offered to its readers. The Separatists had studied their Bible too carefully not to

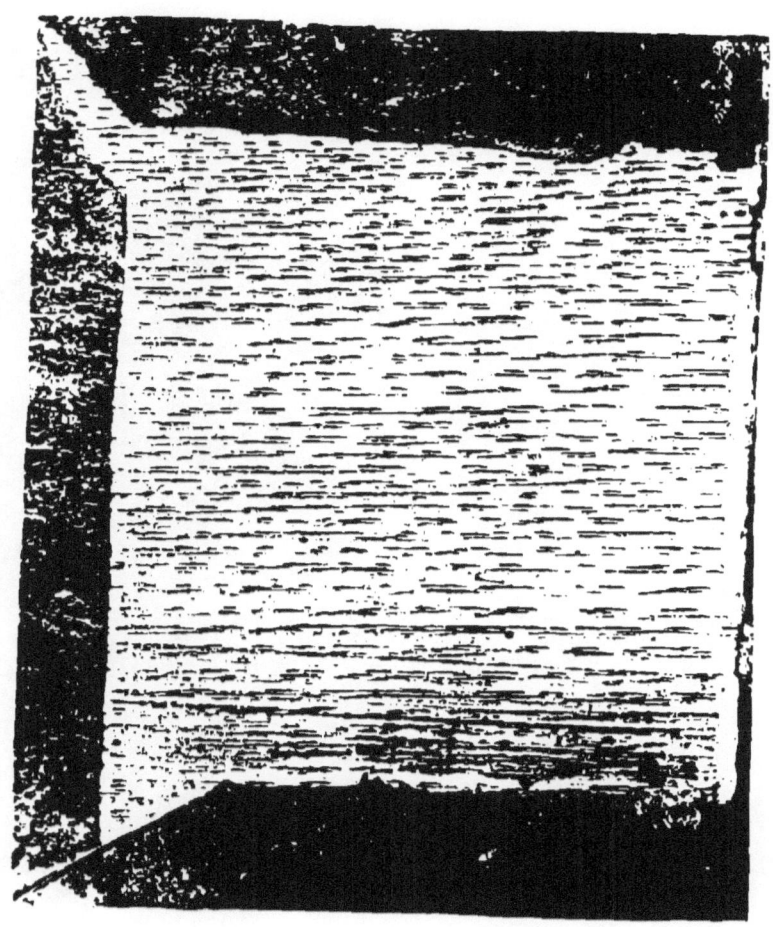

Inside Binding of the "New England Primer" (Boston: 1762)

know that a future life of bliss was far more an instinctive longing of mankind than an Old Testament promise. They were too imbued with the faith of Judaism not to preach a religion of stern justice, and the oldest Puritan literature and even laws read strangely Hebraic to nineteenth century eyes. The religion of Christ, a faith based on love and mercy, received less sympathy and less teaching, from their divines than probably from any other sect nominally Christian. Salvation from hell was what they promised; while, to make this boon the greater, the horrors and tortures were magnified and dwelt upon; and that the terror might be the greater, God was made sterner and more cruel than any living judge, that all might be brought to realize how slight a chance even the least erring had of escaping eternal damnation.

But in this very accentuation of the danger lay the strength of Puritanism. No mass or prayer, no priest or pastor, stood between man and his Creator, each soul being morally responsible for its own salvation; and this tenet forced every man to think, to read, to reason. As the Reformation became possible only when the Bible was cheapened by printed versions, so the moment each man could own and study the Book, Puritanism began. Unless, however, man could read, independence was impossible, for illiteracy compelled him to rely upon another for his knowledge of the Word; and thus, from its earliest inception, Puritanism, for its own sake, was compelled to foster education. Probably no better expression of this fact can be found than in an order of the " General Corte" of the Colony of the Massachusetts Bay, in 1647, that:

" It being one cheife piect of y^t ould deluder, Satan, to keepe men from the knowledge of y^e Scriptures, as in form^r times by keeping y^m in an unknown tongue, so in these latt^r times by pswading from y^e use of tongues, y^t so at least y^e true sence & meaning of y^e originall might be clouded by false glosses of saint seeming deceivers, y^t learning may not be buried in y^e grave of o^r fath^rs in y^e church & comonwealth, the Lord assisting o^r endeavo^rs, —

It is therefore ord'ed, y^t ev^ry towneship in this iurisdiction, aft^r y^e Lord hath increased y^m to y^e number of 50 household^rs, shall then forthw^th appoint one w^ll in their

*Resolve of the General Court of the Massachusetts Bay in 1647*

towne to teach all such children as shall resort to him to write & reade." [1]

*Danger of Independency and Necessity for Conformity*

Independency, no less than Papacy and Episcopacy, was able to foresee the danger of individualism in that it threatened to result in a man's not finding in the Bible the one belief by which alone the Puritans held he could be saved. Think for himself he must, but it was his duty to think what the Separatists thought, and so churches were gathered, and "teachers" — as they were first called — were chosen, who told their congregations what they were to think for themselves. Very quickly organized sects followed, which formulated creeds and catechisms, demanded belief in them, and

---

[1] "Records of the Massachusetts Bay," II., 203.

tortured, imprisoned and exiled the recalcitrant. Finding that other men, like themselves, could not be made by punishment to accept other than their own opinions, the children were taken in their earliest years,[1] and drilled and taught to believe what they were to think out for themselves when the age of discretion was reached. And this was the function of the New England Primer. With it millions were taught to read, that they might read the Bible; and with it these millions were catechised unceasingly, that they might find in the Bible only what one of many priesthoods had decided that book contained.

---

[1] John Trumbull, the poet, records of himself that "before he was two years old, [he] could say by heart all the verses in the 'Primer.'"

*Romish Abece-
dariums and
Prymers*

THIS method of securing uni-
formity by uniting alphabet
and creed was as old as printed
books. The Enschedé Abecedarium,
which has even been claimed to be the
first specimen of printing with type,
and which certainly was printed in the
fifteenth century,[1] contained besides
the alphabet, the Pater Noster, the Ave
Maria, the Credo, and two prayers,
being the elementary book of the Romish Church. So too, a larger book
of Catholicism, for more advanced
students, was the well-known " Book
of Hours " ; which, translated from the
Latin text into English,[2] was called
" The Prymer of Salisbury use ", and
was printed as early as 1490. As

[1] De Vinne's " Invention of Printing," 290.
[2] " The Prymer of Salysbury use." Paris : 1490.

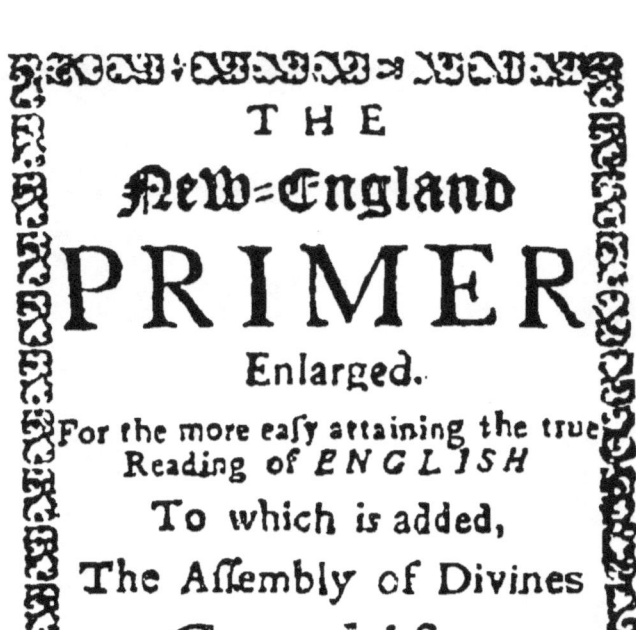

# THE
## New-England
# PRIMER
Enlarged.

For the more eafy attaining the true
Reading of *ENGLISH*

To which is added,

The Affembly of Divines

## Catechifm.

---

BOSTON: Printed by T. Fleet,
and Sold by the bookfellers, 1737.

need hardly be said there are many later editions of both these works.

When the Reformation began to work among the people in England, among its signs was the appearance of unauthorized primers, and Henry the VIII. issued "proclamations" and "injunctions" against these, in an endeavor to keep his people true to Catholicism. Very soon, however, he experienced a change of heart not merely towards his wedded wife, but incidentally as well, towards his mother church, and in 1534, as one method of fighting the Pope, he allowed to be prepared and issued what is known as the "Reform Primer",[1]

*Henry VIIItb's Prymers and A B Cs*

---

[1] "A Prymer in Englyshe with certeyne prayers and goodly meditations, very necessary for all people that understonde not the Latyne tongue. Cum privilegio Regali." [London, 1534.]

designed to teach his people what they should believe. In this, however, his desire to have done with the Church of Rome, led him to act too hastily, for in less than a year, he varied his belief and licensed the issue to his people of a " Goodly Prymer in Eng-lysshe "[1] that they might know the only true and revised-to-date religion. Yet again new light came to the head of the English church, and in a third primer, known as the " Henry VIIIth Primer ",[2] the King marked out

[1] " A goodly Prymer in Englysshe, newly corrected and printed, with certeyne godly Meditations and Prayers added to the same, very necessarie and profitable for all them that ryghte assuredly understande not ye Latine and Greke tongues. Cum privilegio regali." [London, 1535.]

[2] " The Primer set forth by th· King's Majesty, and his Clergy to be taught, learned, and read and none other be used throughout all his dominions. 1545. Cum privilegio ad imprimendum solum."

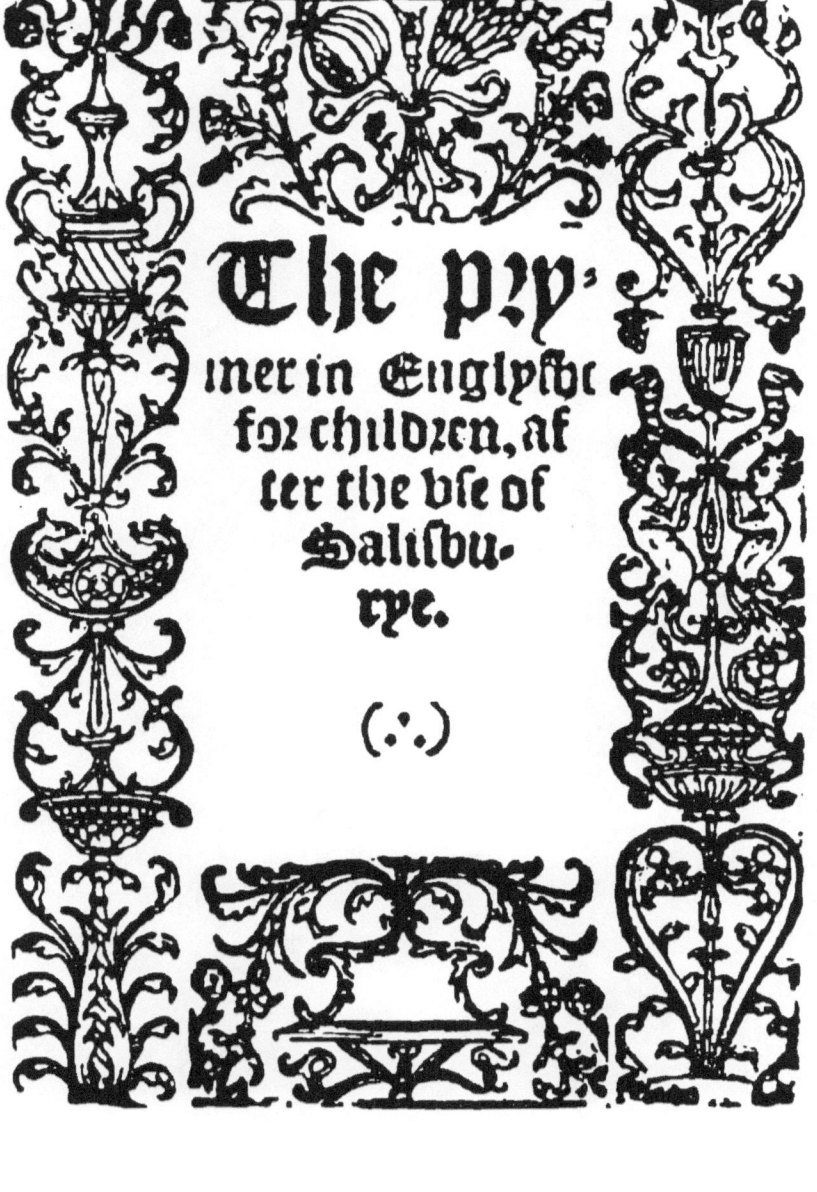

# The pry=
iner in Englysic
for children, af
ter the vse of
Salisbu=
rye.

(∴)

a new and only path to heaven for his subjects. All these primers contained portions intended for " beginners ", such as " a fruitful and very Christian instruction for children ", and since the Romish Church had a preliminary book to its Prymer, so Henry had his, called " The A B C ",[1] the earliest known copy of which contains the alphabet, the Lord's Prayer, the Hail Mary, the Creed, various Graces for before and after " dyner " and for " fysshe dayes ", and the " ten comaundements ". The distinction between the two was well indicated by a little poem at the end of the A B C [2] printed in black letter in 1636:

---

[1] " The A B C bothe in Latyn and in Englysh." [London, 1538.]

[2] " The A B C. The Catechism : That is to say,

*This little Catechisme learned
by heart ( for so it ought )
The Primer next commanded is
for Children to be taught.*

*Spread of dis-
sent and di-
versity of
Primers*
As was not surprising, many of the King's subjects became somewhat unsettled in their belief, and even developed a tendency to form one not ordained by his majesty. Furthermore these wayward people declined to use the primers printed " cum privilegio regali " but purchased heretical books put forth without authority, so that Henry in the preface of his later primers, took notice in evident disgust " of the diversitie of primer books that ar now abrod, whereof ar almost

An Instruction to be taught and learned of every Childe, before he be brought to be confirmed by the Bishop.'' [London ? 1636.]

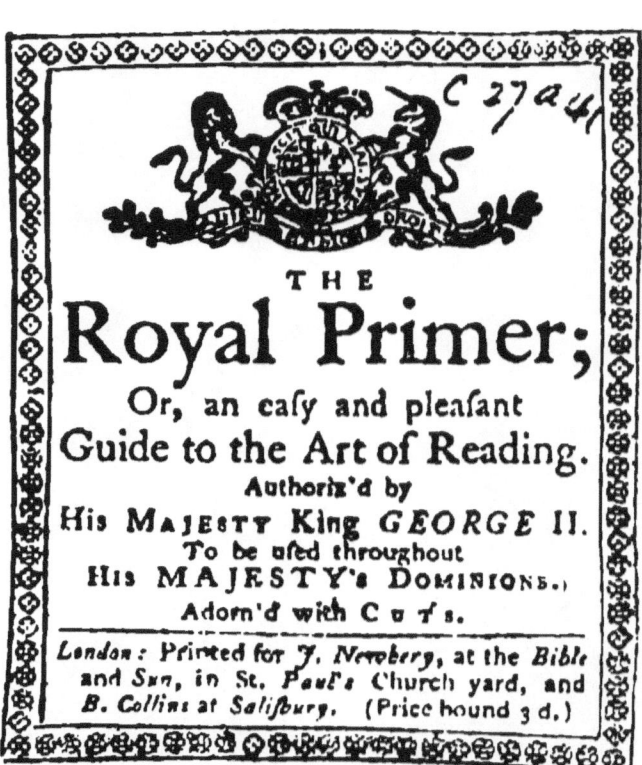

THE

# Royal Primer;

Or, an eafy and pleafant
Guide to the Art of Reading.
Authoriz'd by
His MAJESTY King *GEORGE* II.
To be ufed throughout
His MAJESTY's DOMINIONS.
Adorn'd with Cuts.

London: Printed for *J. Newbery*, at the *Bible*
and *Sun*, in St. *Paul's* Church yard, and
*B. Collins* at *Salisbury*. (Price bound 3 d.)

# A GUIDE.

## FOR THE

## *Child* and *Youth*.

### In Two Parts.

*The First, for* CHILDREN:
Containing plain and pleasant Directions
to read ENGLISH.
With Prayers, Graces, and Instructions
fitted to the Capacity of Children.

### *The Second, for* YOUTH:

Teaching to Write, Cast Account. and
Read more perfectly.
With several other Varieties, both
pleasant and profitable.

*by* T. H. *M. A. Teacher of a private School*

*London :* Printed by *J. Roberts*, for the
Company of Stationers. 1725.

innumerable sortes, which mynister
occasion of contentions and vain dis-
putations, rather then to edify". To
end this difficulty he commanded
" one uniforme ordre of al such bookes
throughout al our dominions, both to
be taught unto children and also to be
used for ordinary prayers of all our
people not learned in the latyn tong",
and for that purpose,

" set furth thys Primer or boke of prayers
in Englysh to be frequented and used in *Henry*
and throughout all places of oure said realmes *VIIItb's*
and dominions, as well of the elder people, *injunction*
as also of the youth, for their common *concerning*
and ordinary prayers, willing, commaund- *Primers*
yng and streghtly chargyng that for the
better bringing up of youth in the knowledge of theyr duty towardes God, their
prince, and all others in their degre, every
Scholemaster and bringer-up of yong begin-

ners in lernyng nexte after their A B C now bi us also set furthe, do teache this primer or boke of ordinary prayers unto them in Englyshe, and that the youth customably and ordinarily use the same until thei be of competant understanding and knowledge to perceive it in Latyn. At which time they may at their libertie either use this primer in Englishe, or that whiche is by oure authoritie likewyse made in the Latyn tong, in all poinctes correspondent unto this in Englysche." [1]

*Multiplica-tion of creeds and cate-chisms*This injunction it is needless to say was little heeded. The English King could depose the vicegerent of Heaven, even though the latter was infallible, but he could not overcome the common people. Faiths and Creeds mul-

[1] "The Prymer both in Englishe and Latin." [London, 1545.]

tiplied until the famous Council of Trent complained of the "infinite" number of the "little books" and complained that there had come to be " as many catechisms as there are provinces in Europe, nay, almost as many as the cities, are circulated, all of which abound with heresies, whereby the minds of the simple are deceived." Their majesties Henry, Edward, Mary, Elizabeth and James, though each having a different faith, successively forbade, seized and burned these unauthorized books; and whipped, imprisoned or burned preachers and printers, but it was all unavailing, and a little over a century and a half from the time that Henry changed the religion of his country, the people decided that it was easier to change their King than to conform in their religion. With the flight of James II. ended all attempts to prevent the people from having such primers and catechisms as they chose, leaving behind nothing but a restriction in the printing of the Bible and the Book of Common Prayer, which to this day are monopoly books in Great Britain.

\* \*

*Authorized and unauthorized Primers and A B C*

THE authorized primers were not true school-books, being rather primary — hence "primer" — manuals of church service, and indeed the forerunners of the "Book of Common Prayer". Moreover they were handsomely printed, and thus were expensive. The authorized

A B C, which sold at a moderate price, contained but the most elementary matter. It must have very quickly occurred to booksellers that to combine the two into one work would be a good idea, but as they were both monopoly books most printers were debarred from doing it and to the privileged printers there was no object in producing them at a low price. It was left, therefore, to the publishers of Separatist persuasion, to take advantage of the larger sale that could be obtained, and very quickly they were issuing at low prices, books which contained the sum of both; and no doubt this cheapness and convenience played a prominent part in the spread of dissent. It was this union of the A B C and the Primer, which

2

led to children's books being called by the latter title.

The earliest of this combination of school-book and catechism, so far discovered, is Bastingius' "Catechisme of Christiane Religion, taught in scholes", which had the A B C prefixed to it, and was printed in Edinburgh in 1591. In 1631 Bishop Bedell's catechism was printed in Dublin, in the same manner. "The A B C. The Catechism: That is to say, an instruction to be taught and learned of every Childe" was printed in 1636. Ten years later the "Catechism for young Children appointed by act of the Church of Scotland" was issued with the A B C, probably in Edinburgh. In England more care had to be taken,

for as late as 1666, one Benjamin
Keach was tried for writing " The
Child's Instructor, or a New and
Easy Primer", which contained a
catechism with leanings towards ana-
baptism; but though the author was
sentenced to the pillory, the book
was constantly republished. A little
later, in 1670, George Foxe issued
his " Primer and Catechism " " with
several delightful Things " intended
to make a Quaker of the student.

One of the gravest difficulties to
the early Separatists in both Old and
New England, was the question of
what catechism to teach their children. During the voyage of the
Arbella the Puritans were catechised
by their clergyman on Sunday, while
no sooner were they landed than the

*The early
catechising of
the New
Englanders*

Colony of Massachusetts Bay made a contract with sundry "intended ministers" for "catechising, as also in teaching, or causing to be taught the Companyes servants & their children, as also the salvages and their children",[1] and in this same year (1629) they voted the sum of three shillings for " 2 dussen and ten catechismes ".[2] It cannot certainly be known to what particular catechism these allusions refer, but it was probably the one composed by "that famous divine" William Perkins, preacher of St. Andrews Church in Cambridge, catechist for some time of Christ college, and one of the most distinguished Calvinists of the

[1] " Records of Massachusetts Bay," I., 37e.
[2] *Ibid*, I., 3-h.

period. First printed in 1590,[1] this catechism ran through many editions in England, was republished with additions by John Robinson for the use of the pilgrims, and later was reprinted in New England.

Very quickly after the Puritan settling in America a tendency developed towards the individualism implied by all dissent and especially by Congregationalism. As a result of this diversity of belief, Lechford states that catechising was generally abandoned in many of the New England churches, and to meet the woeful condition the " General Corte " in 1641 " desired that the elders would make a Catechisme for the

*Neglect of the Catechism in New England*

---

1 " The Foundations of Christian Religion, gathered into sixe Principles. Printed by Thomas Orwin for John Porter, 1590."

instruction of youth in the grounds of religion ",[1] as well as consider "howe farr the magistrates are bound to interfere for the preservacon of that vniformity & peace of the churches ".

*Multiplication of Catechisms*

The request was only too readily responded to and in the period of 1641–1684 the reverend " teachers " Hugh Peters, Edward Norris, Ezekiel Rogers, John Davenport, John Cotton, John Eliot, Thomas Shepard, Richard Mather, John Fiske, John Norton, Seaborn Cotton, James Fitch, Samuel Danforth, James Noyes, and Samuel Stone, each prepared one or more catechisms. In fact it is probable that every New England minister formulated his own faith in this manner, and at first thought it would

[1] " Records of Massachusetts Bay," i., 328.

seem to have been not a little trying
to a congregation, on the death of
a trusted shepherd who had properly
inducted them in his own belief, to
get accustomed to the doctrines of
a new incumbent. This difficulty
was for the most part avoided by
the general knowledge of what each
clergyman thought, so that only one
in fairly close accord with the congregation was considered. When a
mistake occurred, and the " Teacher "
was found to run counter to his
church, they hastened to get rid of
him, which resulted in the innumerable church quarrels and the schism
with which New England so abounded.

Long after Cotton Mather asserted
with evident pride that " few Pastors
of Mankind ever took such pains at

*Resulting quarrels and schisms until the adoption of the shorter Catechism*

*Catechising* as have been taken by our New English Divines : Now, let any Man living read the most judicious and elaborate Catechisms published, a lesser and a larger by Mr. Norton, a lesser and a larger by Mr. Mather, several by Mr. Cotton, one by Mr. Davenport, one by Mr. Norris, one by Mr. Noyes, one by Mr. Fisk, several by Mr. Eliot, one by Mr. Seaborn Cotton, a large one by Mr. Fitch ; and say whether true Divinity were ever better handled."[1] As a fact, however, this very multiplicity of catechisms tended only to increase the schism and the New English clergy spent their energies in preparing catechisms and quarrelling over them rather than in attempting the

---

[1] Mather's Magnalia, book 5, p. 3.

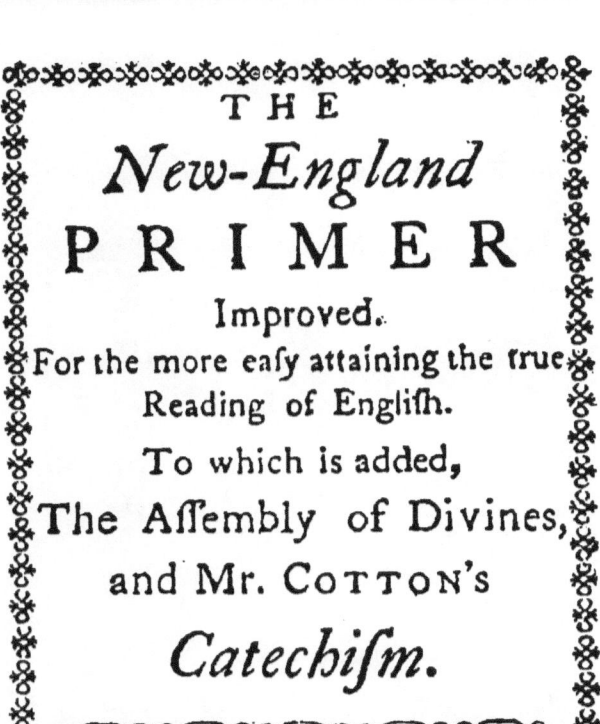

# THE
## *New-England*
# PRIMER

Improved.

For the more eafy attaining the true
Reading of Englifh.

To which is added,

The Affembly of Divines,

and Mr. COTTON's

## *Catechifm.*

*BOSTON:* Printed and Sold by
S. ADAMS, in *Queen-ftreet.* 1762.

" instruction of youth " and the " vniformity and peace of the churches ".
John Cotton, though responsible himself for so much of the disputation,
was forced to acknowledge that " the
excellent and necessary use of catechising young men, and novices, . . .
we willingly acknowledge : But little
benefit have wee seene reaped from
set forms of questions, and answers
by one Church, and imposed by
necessity on another ".[1]  Not till the
great Westminster Assembly formulated its longer and shorter catechisms,
did the New England Churches find
a common faith, and even then, as the
work of Presbyterians and not Con-
gregationalists, they were accepted

---

[1] Cotton's " A Modest and Cleere Answer to Mr.
Ball's Discourse."  London, 1642.

only by degrees, not because they were generally approved, but because they were the only escape from a tendency that threatened to break each congregation into fractions too small for existence as a church.

\* \* \*

SUCH was the condition of school-books and catechisms, when the New England Primer was first published. Its authorship and date of issue have hitherto been mysteries which have resisted the research of all antiquarians, but it is at last possible to give the main facts concerning its origin.

In the reign of King Charles of "merrie" memory, one Benjamin

The New
England
Primer

Harris began printing in London " at the Stationers Arms in Sweethings Rents, near the Royal Exchange ", otherwise described as " the Stationers Arms under the Piazza in Cornhill ". Here he issued, between the years 1676 and 1681 many tracts and broadsides of so little moment that his name finds no mention in any biographical dictionary or history of printing. But aside from his calling, Harris deserves notice as a confirmed scribbler, resembling Mr. Wegg, in his tendency to drop into verse. To this was added an ardent love for the protestant religion, and an equal hatred of the Pope and all that he implied.

So long as the printer limited his activity to the writing and printing of ballads and tracts against the Pope and

*Benjamin Harris, Printer*

*Harris brought to trial*

the Jesuits under such titles as " The Grand Imposter " and " The Mystery of Iniquity," all went well with him, but in 1679, in connection with the " Rye House Plot " he issued " An Appeal from the Country to the City, for the Preservation of His Majesties Person and the Protestant Religion ". The King's government did not take the same view of the question that Mr. Harris had, and as a result he was brought to trial for the " printing and vending " of this tract. The courtly tendency towards Catholicism gave little chance for the printer, and the chief justice, after remarking that if he had his wish, the printer should be whipped, ordered him to find security for his good behavior for three years.[1]

[1] " A short account of the tryal of B. Harris," London : 1679.

Unwarned by his experience, Harris in 1681 printed a " Protestant Peti- *Sentenced to* tion ", and was once more haled before *the pillory* the court and this time the judge fined him five hundred pounds and ordered him put in the pillory. This meant that he was to be stoned by the crowd which always gathered, but from that fate he was saved, for " his Wife (like a Kind Rib) stood by him to defend her Husband against the Mobb ". [1] For this act, his enemies promptly turned their abuse upon the woman, and scurrilous ballads entitled " The Saint turned Courtezan " and the " Protestant Cuckold " endeavored to bring discredit upon her. The printer apparently could not pay the mulct, for he was " for above two years a

[1] Dunton's " Letters from New England," 143.

Prisoner ", and he seems to have ceased printing from that time.

*Removes to Boston in New England*

Upon the death of Charles II. and the succession of Catholic James " Old England ", wrote John Dunton from Boston, " is now so uneasie a Place for honest Men, that those that can will seek out for another Countrey: And this I suppose is the Case of Mr. Benjamin Harris and the two Mr. Hows, whom I hear are coming hither and to whom I wish a good Voyage. Mr. Ben Harris, you know, has been a noted Publick Man in England, and I think the Book of English Liberties . . . was done for him and Mr. How : No wonder then that in this Reign they meet with Enemies ". [1]

[1] Dunton's " Letters from New England," 144.

Come to Boston Harris did and late in 1686 he set up a book and " Coffee, Tee and Chucaletto " shop,[1] by the " Town-Pump near the Change ". A year later his imprint reads " at the London Coffee House " and he was employing the printers of the town to print pamphlets and broadsides for him. Here too he was quickly involved with the authorities, for in 1690 he issued, without permission, the first newspaper printed in America, under the title of " Public Occurrences "; which was promptly suppressed by proclamation. In 1691 he formed a partnership with John Allen, and seems to have set up a press of his own. A year later he became " Printer to His Excellency the Governor and Council ", and re-

*Sets up a book-shop and coffee-house*

---

[1] " Boston Town Records," 204.

moved his business to a "Shop, over against the Old-Meeting House", making another remove in 1694 to a place which he called "The Sign of the Bible, over against the Blew-Anchor", having ended his relations with Allen.

*Returns to England and resumes printing*

In the meantime the English people had stood firm to their religion and had rid themselves of their king, so that now Old England was once more safe to haters of popery. Better still, King William, whose advent Harris hailed in a poem beginning:

> "God *SAVE THE KING*, *that King that sav'd the land*,
> *When JAMES your Martyr's Son, your LAWS had shamm'd.*" [1]

had freed the press from the worst features of governmental restraint.

[1] "Monthly Observations," Boston : 1692.

Accordingly, Harris returned to London towards the end of 1695, and opened a new printing office at the " Maiden-Head-Court in Great East Cheap ", and later Dunton writes that he " continu'd Ben Harris still; and is now both Bookseller and Printer, in Grace-church Street, as we find by his *London Post ;* so that his conversation is general (but never Impertinent) and his Wit pliable to all Inventions. But yet his vanity (if he has any) gives no Alloy to his Wit, and is no more than might justly Spring from conscious Vertue ; and I do him but Justice in this part of his Character, for in once travelling with him from Bury Fair, I found him to be the most Ingenious and Innocent Companion that I had ever met with ".[1]

[1] Dunton's " Life and Errors."

3

When Harris died cannot be discovered, but it was after 1716.

\*
\* \*

BEFORE his flight in 1686 to Boston (according to Dunton) "Mr. Harris I think also Printed the Protestant Tutor, a Book not at all relish'd by the Popish Party, because it is the design of that little Book to bring up Children in an Aversion to Popery". It was first advertised in Harris's newspaper Feb. 27, 1679, and in it lay the germ of the New England Primer. Here was the usual portrait of the reigning sovereign as a frontispiece, and portions of the text were the "Roman Small Letters", the Syllabarium, the Lord's Prayer, the

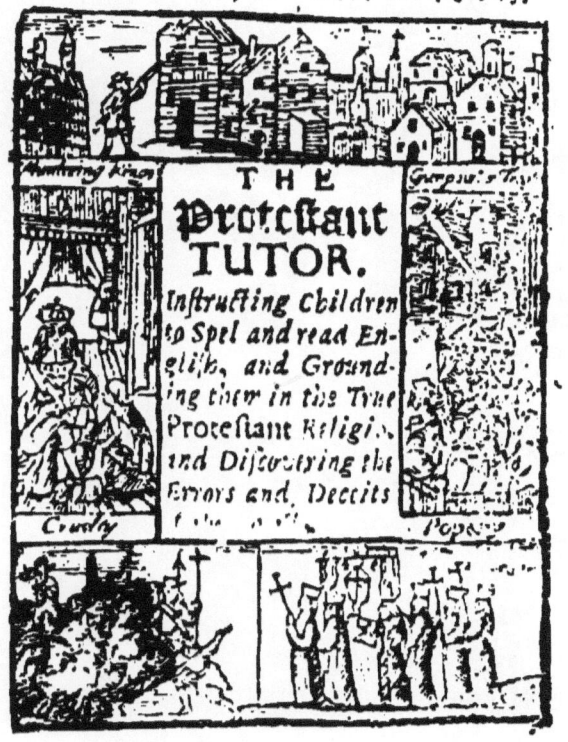

Creed, the Ten Commandments, the
John Rogers biography and verses,
though not the famous picture of the
martyr at the stake, the words of
from two to seven syllables, the
Proper Names, and a catechism, together with much other material for
the benefit of youth and the injury
of Papacy, the whole being dedicated
"To the Right Honourable *James*,
Earl of Doncaster and Dalkeith,
Eldest Son of the Illustrious *Protestant* Prince *James* Duke of Mon-
mouth" by "Your Lordships most
Humble Servant, Benjamin Harris."
The preface, addressed "To all Protestant Parents, School-Masters, and
School Mistresses of Children" "in-
forms" them "*that this little book may
in some measure discover to our children*

what they must certainly expect if ever *Popery* prevail against us, and therefore nothing can be thought more necessary than to teach them to *Spell* and *Read* English, and to Create in them an Abhorrence of Romish *Idolatry* at the same time, which being inspired in their green and tender years, may leave an Impression in their *Minds* to the *End* of their *Lives*, which is the *Real* and *Hearty Desire* and *Design of,* Your Friend and Servant, Benj. Harris."

*Success of The Protestant Tutor*

Apparently this appeal to parents and teachers bore fruit, for on Feb. 1, 1680, the printer announced a second impression, though the price was lowered from eight to six pence. At the time Harris was arrested some five hundred copies of the book, presumptively of this new edition, were seized and taken from him. In 1685 it was reissued, probably in an abridged form, in Boston, and it was once again printed by Harris in London, in 1695, the advertisement of this edition describing it as "A Little Book of Martyrs with pictures for enlivening every History; which book formerly found such General Acceptance that many thousand of them were sold, and it is now reduced to so low a rate that parents may both delight and profit there [*sic*] Children at Three-pence or Four-pence charge and thereby contribute toward the Suport of him who is their Hearty Friend and Servant, Benjamin Harris." In an enlarged form the work was again issued in London in 1715, and its compiler printed a new edition in 1716.

Ere this, in 1686, Harris had sought refuge in New England. On his setting up in Boston as a bookseller it was obviously to his interest to get out a new edition of the little book, for its chance of success among the popery-hating New Englanders was even greater than that it had already met with in Old England. The poverty of the people made prudent an abridgment of the "Tutor" and thus it was reduced to smaller bulk; to make it the more salable the school-book character was increased, while to give it an even better chance for success by an appeal to local pride, it was rechristened and came forth under the now famous title.

No copy of this first edition of the New England Primer is known and thus the exact date of its appearance

## DECEMBER hath 31 Days

Laſt quart. 2 day 24 min. paſt 4 morn.
New Moon 9 day 21 min. paſt 9 morn.
Firſt quart. 17 day 13 min. paſt 2 Afern.
Full Moon 25 day 39 min. paſt 10 night.
Laſt quart. 31 day 59 min. paſt 11 morn

*Of Stars which have appeared heretofore, and now diſappear.*

Time out of mind there has ſeven Stars bin obſerved in the pleiades, and at Preſent there is to be ſeen but ſix, a very probable ſign that one of them is retired and become inviſible. One of theſe of the Conſtellation of the *Little Bear*, which was formerly viſible, doth not now appear. Another alſo in the Conſtellation of *Andromeda* hath alſo diſappeared.

*Licens'd according to Order.*

## ADVERTISEMENT.

There is now in the Preſs, and will ſuddenly be extant, a Second Impreſſion of *The New-England Primer enlarged*, to which is added, more *Directions for Spelling* : the *Prayer of* K Edward the 6th. and *Verſes made by Mr.* Rogers *the Martyr, left as a Legacy to his Children.*

Sold by *Benjamin Harris*, at the *London Coffee-Houſe* in *Boſton*.

First Mention of the " New England Primer "

(From " Newman's News from the Stars." Boston : 169

cannot be given. Harris did not ar-
rive in Boston till near the end of
1686, and the only publication he
issued in that year was an almanac
for 1687, which Sewall bought on
December 6, 1686. Between that
time and Jan. 5, 1688, Harris made
a trip to England, and on Nov. 22,
1688 he again sailed for London.[1]  It
was between 1687 and 1690, therefore, that the first edition of the Primer
was issued.  Its success seems to have
been immediate, for in Henry Newman's almanac entitled " News from
the Stars ", " Printed by R. Peirce
for Benjamin Harris at the London
Coffee-House in Boston, 1691 " (and
consequently printed late in 1690)
the last leaf advertised a " second Im-

*Date of pub-
lication, and
advertisement
of the second
impression*

---

[1] Sewall's " Diary," I., 200, 237.

pression of *The New England Primer,*
Enlarged ".

A very essential piece of evidence
in regard to the date of the book is
connected with the earliest (supposed)
fragment of the Primer known. This
consists of four leaves, and was found
bound up as waste in the binding of a
copy of Daniel Leeds' "Temple of
Wisdom" as printed by William
Bradford at Philadelphia in 1688.
From this it has been argued that
"these leaves probably came from a
Philadelphia reprint of a Boston edition of the Primer which must have
been published at least as early as
1687". The evidence of this does
not seem adequate. There is no
proof that the volume was bound in
the year that it was printed, nor can

it be decided for certain that the fragments are a reprint of the Primer, the
chances being quite as favorable of
their being part of an edition of the
Protestant Tutor. All that can be
said of these leaves is that they are
the earliest known fragments of a book
compiled by Benjamin Harris, and that
they were printed by William Bradford either in Philadelphia or New
York between 1687 and 1700. From
other facts known of Bradford this
was presumably a stealing of Harris's
book and is therefore an early American case of literary theft.

The book proved so great a success
in New England that when its compiler returned to Old England, he
continued to publish it. In a work [1]

[1] Davenport's " Saints Anchor hold." London :
1701.

printed by him in 1701 is advertised at the end, among other "Books Printed and Sold by B. Harris at the Golden Boar's-Head in Grace-church St.", "The *New* England Primer Enlarged; For the more easy attaining the true Reading of English. To which is added *Milk* for *Babes.*" He seems to have also published editions of it under a title which would make it more attractive to the English public, for in the reign of Queen Anne (1702–1714) he issued what is presumably the same text as his New England Primer, under the title of "The New English Tutor". But the other title proved the more popular, and under it numerous editions were printed in England and Scotland, even into the nineteenth century.

THE
*New Englifh*
TUTOR,
*Enlarged* ;
For the more eafy
attaining the True
Reading of
ENGLISH,
To which is added
*Milk for Babes*

I    VI
II   VII
III  VIII
IV   IX
V    X

It was in New England, however, that its great success was achieved. Primer to printer and people there soon meant only the New England Primer, all other varieties being specially designated to show that they were not of the popular kind. Copies of the little book were as much a matter of "stock" in the bookshops of the towns and general stores of the villages as the Bible itself. In the inventory of Michael Perry, a Boston bookseller, filed in 1700, is entered "28 Primmers" and "44 doz. Primmers",[1] and standard advertisements in newspapers and books announced that such and such a printer has for sale "Bibles, Testaments, Psalters,

*Success of the Primer in New England*

---

[1] Dunton's "Letters from New England," 316, 318.

Psalm-Books, Primers, Account Books and Books of Record ". Indeed it was so taken for granted that copies were in stock, that many printers and booksellers did not think the fact worth advertising.

*Changes of title*

Occasionally printers in America tried to better the sale by re-naming it, as when Thomas Green issued it in New London with the title of " A Primer for the Colony of Connecticut " and Henry de Forest printed it at New York as " The New York Primer ". When the United States became a fact, it was several times printed under the titles of " The American Primer ", or " The Columbian Primer ". But the variations were not popular, the ventures did not succeed the better, and eventually the

THE

*NEW-ENGLAND*

PRIMER,

Or: an eafy and pleafant

GUIDE to the ART of READING

Adorn'd with CUTTS.

To which are added,

THE ASSEMBLY OF DIVINES'

CATECHISM.

BOSTON :—Printed and fold by
J. WHITE, near Charles-River
Bridge.

" New England Primer " became the deservedly established title.

For one hundred years this Primer was *the* school-book of the dissenters of America, and for another hundred, it was frequently reprinted. In the unfavorable locality (in a sectarian sense) of Philadelphia, the accounts of Benjamin Franklin and David Hall show that between 1749 and 1766, or a period of seventeen years, that firm sold thirty-seven thousand one hundred copies. Livermore stated in 1849 that within the last dozen years " 100,000 copies of modern editions . . . have been circulated ". An over conservative claim for it is to estimate an annual average sale of twenty thousand copies during a period of one hundred and fifty years, or total sales of three million copies.

*Magnitude of sales*

_Rarity of the Primer, and the reasons_

Despite this enormous number, early editions of the New England Primer are among the rarest of school-books. Edward Coote, in his "English Schoole-Master" (London 1597) recommended to purchasers of his book, that :

"If, notwithstanding any former reasons, thou doubtist that thy little child will have spoyled this booke before it bee learned ; thou maist fitly diuide it at the end of the second booke, or thou mayest reserve faire the written copies, vntill he can read."

When to the destruction of the child, is added the slight value set by adults on children's books of their own time, it is not strange that works intended for the instruction or amusement of the young should constitute one of the rarest of all classes of literature.

This destruction and heedlessness has made a study of the New England Primer an almost hopeless undertaking. Eagerly searched for by many collectors in the last fifty years, no copy of a seventeenth century edition of the work has been discovered, and this search has brought to light less than fifty editions and less than sixty copies of New England Primers printed in the eighteenth century. Although as already noted Franklin and Hall printed over thirty-seven thousand copies between 1749 and 1766 (and as Franklin printed an edition as early as 1735 and Hall as late as 1779 it is probable that they issued at least double that number), but a single copy with their imprints is known to exist. Thomas states that

*Difficulty of studying and collecting*

Fowle printed about 1757 one edition of 10,000 copies, but not a single primer with his imprint is extant. This is typical of the majority of the issues. Only twelve copies of editions printed before 1780 have been disposed of at auction in the last twenty years, and they have sold for an average of one hundred dollars each.

\* \*
\*

*Variations of Primer*

ALTHOUGH each printer of the New England Primer changed title and text to suit his taste or business interests, certain unmistakable ear-marks, or what the naturalist would term "limit of organic variation", serve to mark beyond question every edition of the

Primer, however titled or altered. The printers of other school-books often inserted fragments of the more famous Primer in their ventures, but this deceived neither the public then nor the book lover now, the true Primer being too sharply differentiated from all others for there to be the possibility of confusion.

Every New England Primer, like many others, began with the letters *The alphabet* of the alphabet, followed by various *and syllaba-* repetitions making clear the distinc- *rium* tions between vowels, consonants, double letters, italic and capitals. After this came what was called "Easy Syllables for Children," or as it was frequently termed, the "sylla-barium," beginning with such combinations as "ab, eb, ib, ob, ub,"

4

followed by words of one syllable
which lengthened by degrees to im-
posing vocables of six syllables. It
is to be noted however, that occasionally when the printer was cramped
for space, he limited the ambition of
the student by dropping out these
polysyllabic words, and gave only
the shorter ones. This whole elementary section of the primer had
been used in Coote's "The English
Schoolmaster," as early as 1596, and
may have been framed by him, but
as the first part is practically what
went to make the Horn-Book of the
period, its antiquity may be far greater
than Coote's book.

One apparently trivial distinction
in the text as given in the New
England Primer, yet which had a

*f*

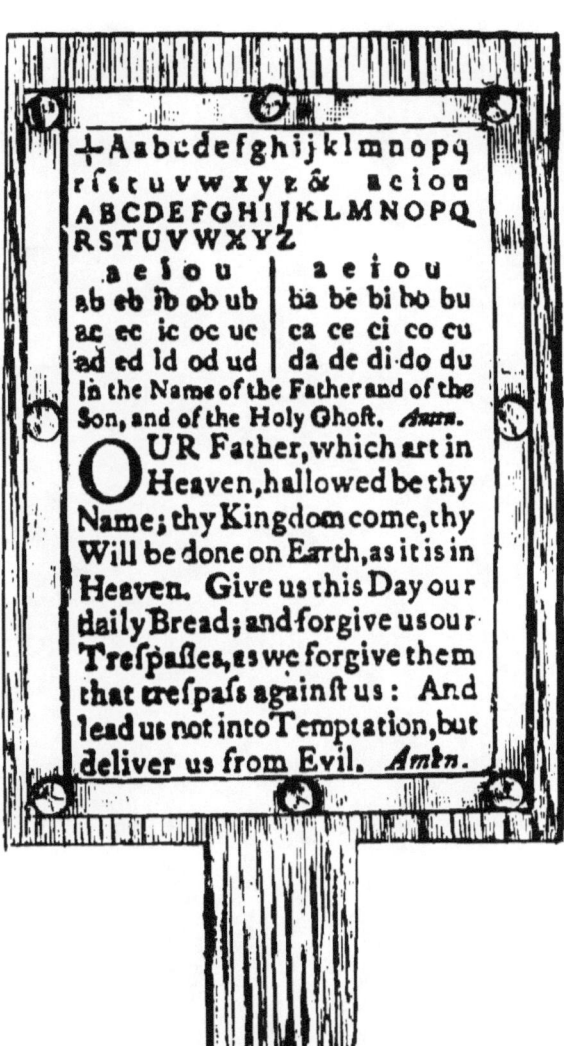

Reproduction of Horn Book

deep motive, is the omission at the beginning of the alphabet of the ✠ The omission which otherwise was so almost in- *of the* ✠ variably placed there, as to give to the first line of the alphabet the name of " Christ's Cross-Row " or as it was more commonly termed " the Cris Cross Row." In Morton's " New English Canaan " he speaks of " a silenced Minister " who came over to New England and brought " a great Bundell of Horne books with him and careful hee was (good man) to blott out all the crosses of them for feare least the people of the land should become Idolaters." Of this Puritan dread of the cross, the New England Primer always took heed, and no edition is known, even in those prepared for Episcopalians, to contain the oldest religious emblem now worshipped.

*Alphabet of lessons* Usually following the syllabarium, was what was called " An Alphabet of Lessons for Youth," being a series of moral and instructive sentences taken from the Bible, so worded and arranged as to begin each paragraph with a successive capital letter of the alphabet, the sole exception being in the case of **X,** for that letter proved beyond the ability of the compiler to find a sentence beginning properly, and he dodged the issue in the following manner

*" eXhort one another daily "*.

*The Lord's Prayer and the Creed* In every " New England Primer " the Lord's Prayer and Apostles' Creed was included, and while their position

A
In *Adam's* Fall
We finned all.

B
Thy Life to mend
This *Book* attend.

C
The *Cat* doth play
And after flay.

D
A *Dog* will Bite
A Thief at Night.

E
An *Eagle*'s Flight
Is out of Sight.

F
An idle *Fool*
Is whipt at School.

As

Rhymed Alphabet Pages

(From the "New English Tutor." London: [1742-1745?]

G As runs the *Glaſs.*
Man's life doth paſs

H My *Book* and *Heart*
Shall never part.

J Sweet *Jeſus* He
Dy'd on a Tree.

K K. *William*'s Dead
and left the Throne
To *Ann* our Queen
of great Renown.

L The *Lyon* bold
The *Lamb* does hold

M Moon gives light
In time of Night.

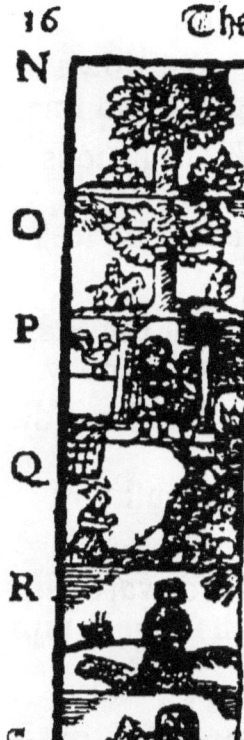

N *Nightingales* fing
in time of Spring.

O The Royal Oak
It was the Tree
That fav'd his
P Royal Majefty.

*Peter* Denies
His Lord and cryes

Q Queen *Efther* came
in Roysl State,
To fave the Jews
R from difmal Fate.

*Rachel* doth mourn
for her firft-born,

S *Samuel* anoints
whom God appoints.

Turn

T  *Time* cuts down all
both great and small

U  *Uriah's* beautious
Wife,
Made *David* seek
his Life.

W  Whales in the Sea,
God's Voice obey.

X  *Xerxes* the Great did
dye,
And so must you
and I

Y  *Youths* forward slips
Death soonest nips.

Z  *Zacheus* he
did climb the Tree,
his Lord to see.

was varied, they commonly followed
the "Alphabet of Lessons."

\* \*
\*

NEXT in order of what went
to make the Primer famous *The Rhymed*
were the twenty-four little *Alphabet*
pictures, with alphabetical rhymes,
commencing

"*In Adam's Fall
We sinned All*".

— A description of the beginning of
original sin which certainly did its
best to balance our first forebears' very
ungenerous version of the affair which
to the Puritan was the greatest event
in history.

This method of teaching the
alphabet by short poems was of much

older date. As early as 1552 there was printed in England a little tract entitled " Alphabetum primum Becardi," which consisted of rhymes to each of the letters, and another work of this period of exactly the same character was entitled " Finch his Alphabet ". So, too, a little later a broadside was issued, headed " All the Letters of the A. B. C. by every sondrye Letter wherof ther is a good Document set fourth and taught in Ryme. Translated out of Bas-Almaine into English, anno 1575 ". An even further development of this was contained in Wastell's " Microbiblion, or the Bibles Epitome"[1] (London 1629) containing the sum of the whole, in verse so capitalized as to form successive alphabets.

[1] An edition with a different title was printed as early as 1623.

Who was the author of the New England Primer alphabet verses is not known, no text of it before its printing in that work having been found. It could not have been written long before the first appearance of that book, for the rhyme:

*Authorship of Rhymed Alphabet*

> " *The Royal Oak*
> *It was the Tree*
> *That sav'd his*
> *Royal Majesty,*"

by its allusion to King Charles, clearly shows it to have been composed after 1660. All this points to the compiler of the Primer as its author, for in other poems he expresses the greatest admiration for the Merrie Monarch, and as already noted, he was continually scribbling verse quite of the character of the rhymed alphabet.

But there is better proof of Harris's authorship than mere inference. A study of the twenty-four rhymes reveals the fact that certain ones of them seem not merely without moral, but without meaning.

> *The Cat doth play
> And after slay*

leaves one very much in doubt as to · what monition is intended to be conveyed, and equally vague is

> *The Lion bold
> The Lamb doth hold*

Still less valuable, however true, is the information that

> *Nightingales sing
> In time of Spring.*

Finally, it would be cruel to even attempt to compute the bewilderment of the Primer's students due to the stanza

1. *The ROSE crop'd by Tooth.*

LOOK in the Morning, and you'll see
the Rose buds to awake,
And from their Beds most fragrantly,
a pleasant Odour make.

And when the Gard'ner to it goes,
it can't his Knife withstand ;
But strait defends this Damask Rose,
to wither in his Hand.

Ah ! gentle Youth, thus strive to crop
from off this Bush a Flower ;
Turn back ; behold ! one ready stands
thy Youth for to devour.

7. *The Nightingale.*

WHen Winter's hoary Frosts retire,
to usher in the Spring,
Up strikes th'harmonious winged Quire,
melodiously to Sing.

Hark, how the well tun'd Nightingale
sounds forth her quav'ring Note,
And warbles out a pleasant Tale,
with Musick in her throat ;

All Life, she flutters in the Bush,
her strenuous Notes to raise,
And whilst her Life doth last, she thus
Chaunts forth her Maker's Praise.
                                    The

13. *The Lyon and Lamb.*

A Lamb, by chance, had gone astray,
And wand'ring thro' a Wood,
A Lyon met in Masquerade,
Who Fauning by him stood.

Good Lyon, ( quoth the Lamb ) I crave,
My Liege will lend an Ear,
And save me from the rav'nous Wolves,
Whose Jaws I daily fear.

Ne'er heed ; I'll see you safe from them :
The Lyon strait did Rore ;
Till to his Den he came, when he
The Lamb in pieces tore.

37. *The Cat and Rats.*

WHen Puss with mewing made the Rats
their Holes quite to forsake,
She reacheth down a Violin
and strait doth Musick make :

At which they came from far and near
dancing with nimble Feet :
But some more wiser than the rest,
found Food and fell to Eat :

The Cat upon those Rats soon seize,
who next unto her were ;
But all the rest escap'd with Cheese,
and other wholesom Fare.
                                    The

Four Pages from Harriss' Fables of Young Æsop
(London: 1700)

*Youths forward slips*
*Death soonest nips.*

All these enigmas are made clear however by an examination of a little volume entitled "The Fables of Young
Æsop, With their Morals. With a
Moral History of his Life and Death.
Illustrated with Forty curious Cuts,
applicable to each Fable."[1]   This
booklet, "Written by B. H." or Benjamin Harris, contains a series of dog-
gerel verses appended to the "curious
cuts" and when Mr. Harris came
to make his alphabet verses for the
Primer, with a frugality of mind that
would have charmed Mr. Gilpin, he
took certain of the illustrations from

---

[1] The earliest known edition is the Fourth, "London, Printed and Sold by Benj. Harris, at the Golden
Boar's Head, in Grace-Church street.   MDCC."

this other book, and by rewriting his rhymes, utilized them anew in the Primer verses.

It is a curious fact that of all these twenty-four stanzas only the first one, relating to Adam, was not at some time varied or changed, and these variations give a curious illustration of some very important alterations of public opinion. Thus in the earliest text extant, at the letter J is given a picture of the crucifixion, with the stanza

> " *Sweet Jesus he*
> *Dy'd on a Tree.*"

And in an English school-book of other character than the Primer, this was unchanged. The Puritan, however, would not tolerate even this use of the cross, and so very quickly the picture was changed to one of Job, and the rhyme to

> " *Job feels the rod*
> *Yet blesses God.*"

Perhaps the most curious change is
that connected with the letter K.
Allusion has been made to Harris's
admiration for King Charles, and there
is good evidence that for this letter
originally there was a picture of that
monarch and the stanza read

> " *King Charles the Good*
> *No Man of Blood.*" [1]

Presently however the King was dead,
and in a little time another king in the
form of William III. for whom Harris
also felt a strong admiration, was reigning over England. Thereupon the
portrait and stanza were presumably
changed by the insertion of one sing-
ing his praises. When William died

[1] Stanza as printed in " A Guide for the Child ".

*From King to Demos*

however Harris did not displace his portrait, but calling into play his poetic fancy, he affixed to the old cut, the lines

" *K. William's Dead*
*and left the throne*
*To Ann our Queen*
*of great Renown* " [1]

This necessity of changing with each new reign seems to have proved a nuisance, and so someone presently hit upon the device of being always in date, by making the rhyme read

" *Our King the good*
*No man of blood.*" [2]

For many years this form was satisfactory, but finally the Americans began to question if after all the King was good.   To meet this doubt,

[1] " New English Tutor ".
[2] " New England Primer," Boston : 1727.

printers easily changed the praise into
admonition by printing

> " *Kings should be good*
> *Not men of blood.*" [1]

Finally washing their hands of mon-
archy, rhyme too was abandoned, and
the stanza became

> " *The British King*
> *Lost States thirteen,*" [2]

varied occasionally by another form
which announced that

> " *Queens and Kings*
> *Are gaudy things.*" [3]

Akin to this in both democratic
sentiment and verse were revised lines *The letter Q*
for Q, to the effect that

> " *Kings and Queens*
> *Lie in the dust.*" [4]

---

[1] " New England Primer," Boston: 1791.
[2] *Ibid.* Philadelphia: 1797.
[3] *Ibid.* Brattleboro: 1825.
[4] *Ibid.* New York: 1819.

In the same manner, the rhyme already quoted, about the royal oak, became unfit poetry for young republicans, and in attempts to vary it wide divergence crept in, resulting in the following forms:

" *The Royal Oak,*
   *our King did save*
*From fatal Stroke*
   *of Rebel Slave.*" [1]

" *If you seek in the forest*
   *The Oak you will see*
*Among all the rest*
   *is the stateliest tree.*" [2]

" *Of sturdy Oak*
   *That Stately tree*
*The ships are made*
   *That sail the sea.*" [3]

" *The Charter Oak*
   *it was the tree*
*That saved to us*
   *our Liberty.*" [4]

" *The Owl at night*
*Hoots out of sight.*" [5]

" *The Oak for shade*
*& strength was made.*" [6]

---

[1] " A Guide for the Child," 1-25?
[2] " New England Primer." Albany: 1818.
[3] *Ibid.* Walpole: 1806.
[4] *Ibid.* Hartford: 18—?
[5] *Ibid.* New York: 1819.
[6] *Ibid.* Brattleboro: 1825.

Another injection of patriotism was made in the letter W.  Originally this was

*The* Primer
*crowns*
*Washington*

" *Whales in the sea*
*God's voice obey.*"

In some editions of the Primers printed after the American Revolution this somewhat difficult rhyme was omitted, and in its place was one of the following

"*Great Washington brave*   "*By Washington*
*His country did save.*" [1]   *Great deeds were done.*"[2]

All the foregoing were haphazard changes by various printers, but a more sweeping alteration was made between 1740 and 1760.  As originally written [3] many of the verses had a decidedly mundane quality, and so

*The Rhymed
Alphabet
Evangelized*

[1] " New England Primer," Brattleboro: 1825.
[2] *Ibid.*   New York: 1794.
[3] *Ibid.*   Boston: 1727.

some New England writer or printer undertook within that period, to evangelize [1] those lines which had an earthly tendency. What was accomplished, is shown in parallel column:

" *The Cat doth play,*
*And after slay.*"

" *Christ crucify'd*
*For sinners dy'd.*"

" *The Dog will bite,*
*A Thief at Night.*"

" *The Deluge drown'd*
*The Earth around.*"

" *An Eagle's flight,*
*Is out of Sight.*"

" *Elijah hid*
*By ravens fed.*"

" *An idle Fool,*
*Is whipt at School.*"

" *The judgement made*
*Felix afraid.*"

" *Our King the good*
*No man of blood.*"

" *Proud Korah's troop*
*Was swallowed up.*"

" *The Lion bold,*
*The Lamb doth hold.*"

" *Lot fled to Zoar,*
*Saw fiery Shower,*
*On Sodom pour.*"

" *The moon gives Light,*
*In time of night.*"

" *Moses was he*
*Who Israel's Host*
*Led thro' the Sea.*"

[1] " New England Primer," Boston: 1762.

# The Child's Guide.

A — In *Adam's* Fall
We finned all.

B — This *Book* attend,
Thy Life to mend.

C — The *Cat* does play,
And after flay.

D — The *Dog* doth bite
A Thief at Night.

E — An *Eagle's* flight
Is out of fight.

Rhymed Alphabet Pages

(From the "Guide for the Child." London : 1725)

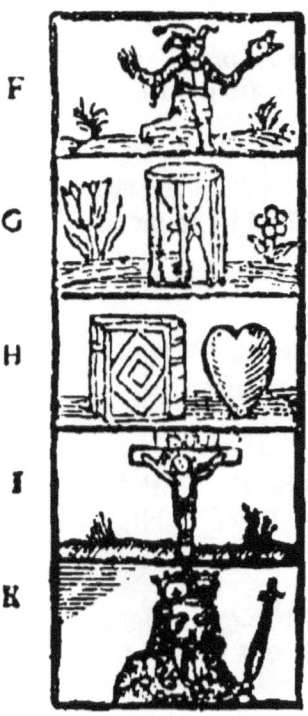

F    The Idle *Fool*
Is whipt at School.

G    As runs the Glafs,
Man's Life doth
pafs.

H    My *Book* and *Heart*
Shall never part

I    *Jefus* did dye
For thee and I

K    King *Charles* the
Good,
No Man of Blood.

A 6        The

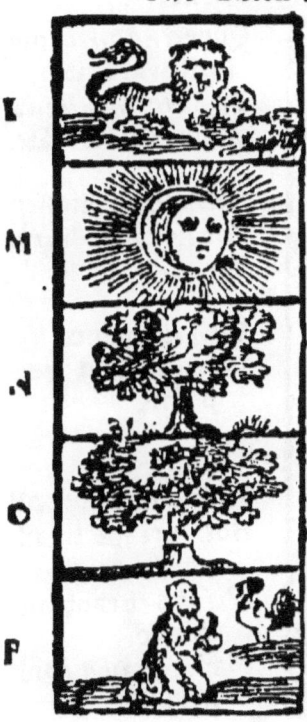

L    The *Lyon* bold,
The *Lamb* doth
    hold.

M    The *Moon* gives
        Light
In time of Night.

N    *Nightingales* fing
In time of Spring.

O    The *Royal Oak*
    our King did fave
From fatal Stroke
    of Rebel Slave.

P    *Peter* denies
His Lord, and cries,

Queen

Q    Queen *Efther* came
in Royal State.
To fave the *Jews*
from difmal Fate.

R    *Rachel* doth mourn
For her firft-born.

S    *Samuel* anoints
Whom God ap-
points.

T    *Time* cuts down all
Both great & small.

U    *Uriah's* beauteous
Wife
Made *David* feek
his Life.

" *Nightingales sing,*
  *In time of Spring.*"

" *Noah did view*
  *The old world & new.*"

" *The Royal Oak,*
  *it was the Tree,*
  *That sav'd his*
  *Royal Majesty.*"

" *Young Obadias,*
  *David, Josias,*
  *All were Pious.*"

" *Rachel doth mourn*
  *For her first born.*"

" *Young Pious Ruth*
  *Left all for Truth.*"

" *Samuel anoints*
  *Whom God appoints.*"

" *Young Sam'l dear*
  *The Lord did fear.*"

" *Time cuts down all,*
  *Both great and small.*"

" *Young Timothy*
  *Learnt Sin to fly.*"

"*Uriah's beauteous Wife,*
*Made David seek his life.*"

" *Vashti for Pride*
  *Was set aside.*"

Much later, in the present century, when children's books began to cater to what a child would like, a reactionary spirit reversed this evangelization and stanzas of worldly tendency were actually inserted in place of them in some editions. These substitution verses were:

*The Rhymed Alphabet modernized*

5

H.  " *Wrote by the hand*
     *Great works do stand.*"

K.  "'*Tis Youth's delight*
     *To fly their kite.*"

R.  " *The Rose in bloom*
     *Sheds sweet perfume.*"

U.  " *Urns hold, we see*
     *Coffee and Tea.*" [1]

The Puritan however did not approve these changes, and they were rarely used.    Nor were the evangelized rhymes ever adopted in Great Britain.

*Minor changes*
*in the Rhymed*
*Alphabet*

Other and less noticeable changes were made, of which the following are the most important that have been found :

" *The Eagle's flight*         " *The Egyptian host*
*Is out of sight.*"           *was in the red sea lost.*" [2]

---

[1] " New England Primer," New York: 1819.
[2] *Ibid.* Wilmington: 1812.

" *Thy life to mend*    " *Heaven to find*
   *This book attend.*" [1]    *The Bible mind.*" [2]

" *Queen Esther came*    " *Queen Esther sues*
      *in royal State,*    *And saves the Jews.*" [2]
*To save the Jews*
   *from dismal Fate.*" [1]

" *Youth's forward slips,*    " *Youth onward slips*
   *Death soonest nips.*" [1]    *Death soonest nips.*"

" *While youth do chear*    " *No Youth we see*
   *Death may be near.*" [2]    *From death is free.*" [3]

" *Xerxes the great did dye*  " *Xerxes did die,*
*And so must you and I.*" [1] *And so must I.*" [2]

There were some few other variations of wording, but of such slight
difference as not to need notice.

1 " New English Tutor."
2 " New England Primer," 1762.
3 " New England Primer."   Brattleboro, 1825.

\*\*\*

EVEN more famous than the rhymed alphabet, is the poem of John Rogers, with the picture of the martyr burning at the stake, and " his Wife, with Nine small Children, and one at her Breast " looking on.   Much sadness this poem and print must have cost the Puritan, and even now, it is capable of producing a sigh, no longer because one feels so keenly for the man, who regardless of wife and children, insisted on being burnt, and really forced the court against its will to make a martyr of him, but because a study of the facts shows that the use of this poem and story was nothing but a piece of sectarian garbling and falsehood, and that all the pity spent upon it by millions of readers was no more deserved than

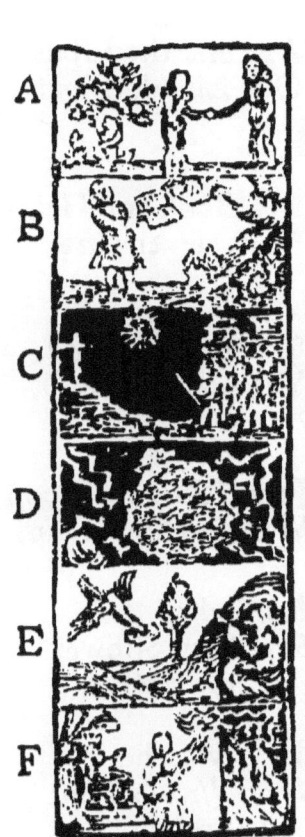

A    In ADAM's Fall,
We sinned all.

B    Heaven to find,
The BIBLE mind.

C    CHRIST crucify'd,
For Sinners dy'd.

D    The Deluge drown'd
The Earth around.

E    ELIJAH hid,
By Ravens fed.

F    The Judgment made
*Felix* afraid.

Rhymed Alphabet Pages

(From the " New England Primer."  Boston : 1762)

**G**  As runs the Glaſs,
Our Life doth paſs.

**H**  My Book and Heart
Muſt never part.

**J**  *Job* feels the Rod,
Yet bleſſes GOD.

**K**  Proud *Korah's* Troop
Was ſwallow'd up.

**L**  *Lot* fled to *Zoar*,
Saw fiery Shower
On *Sodom* pour.

**M**  *Moſes* was he
Who *Iſrael's* Hoſt
Led thro' the Sea.

N    *Noah* did view
The old world & new.

O    Young *Obadias,*
*David, Josias,*
All were pious.

P    *Peter* deny'd
His Lord and cry'd.

Q    Queen *Esther* sues,
And saves the *Jews.*

R    Young pious *Ruth,*
Left all for Truth.

S    Young *Samuel* dear,
The Lord did fear.

**T** Young *Timothy*
Learnt Sin to fly.

**V** *Vaſhti* for Pride,
Was ſet aſide.

**W** Whales in the Sea,
GOD's Voice obey.

**X** *Xerxes* did die,
And ſo muſt I.

**Y** While youth do chear
Death may be near.

**Z** *Zaccheus* he
Did climb the Tree,
Our Lord to ſee.

MR. JOHN ROGERS, Minifter of the
Gofpel in *London*, was the firft Martyr in Queen *Mary's* Reign. and was burnt
at *Smithfield*, February 14th 1554, His
Wife with nine fmall Children, and one
at her Breaft, following him to the Stake;
with which forrowful Sight he was not in
the leaft daunted, but with wonderful Patience died courageoufly for the Gofpel of Jefus
Chrift.                                        *Some*

The Burning of John Rogers

(From the " New England Primer." Boston: 1-62)

that lavished upon the unfortunate heroes and heroines of fiction.

The history of the poem so far as can be learned is as follows. In the sixteenth century there lived a man of whom Foxe, in his " Book of Martyrs," wrote :

" Robert Smith gave himself to service in the house of sir Thomas Smith, knight, being then provost of Eaton : from thence he was preferred to Windsor, having there in the college a clerkship of ten pounds a year. Of stature he was tall and slender, active about many things, but chiefly delighting in the art of painting, which many times rather for his mind's sake, than for any gain, he did practice and exercise. In religion he was fervent, after he had once tasted the truth ; wherein he was much confirmed by the preaching of Mr. Turner, of Windsor, and others. Whereupon at

*Foxe's account of Robert Smith*

the coming of Queen Mary he was de-
prived of his clerkship by her visitors; and
not long after he was apprehended, and
brought to examination before Bonner."

At this point Foxe inserts an account of the trial where Smith

" vailantly stood in defence of his master's
cause: and as thou seest him here boldly
stand in examination before the bishop and
doctors; so was he no less comfortable
also in the prison among his companions:
which also is to be observed no less in his
other fellow-prisoners, who being together
in the outward room in Newgate, had godly
conference with themselves, with daily praying and public reading, which they to their
great comfort used in that room together;
amongst whom Smith was the chief; whose
industry was always solicitous, not only for
them of his own company, but also his
diligence was careful for other prisoners,

whom he ceased not to dissuade from their old accustomed iniquity ; and many he converted to his religion.

"The said Robert Smith, the valiant and constant martyr of Christ, being thus *Burning at* replenished as ye have heard, with the for- *the Stake* titude of God's Spirit, was condemned at London by Bonner their bishop, on the 12th of July ; and suffered at Uxbridge the 8th day of August ; who as he had been before a comfortable instrument of God to all them that were in prison with him : so now also being at the stake, he did no less comfort the people, there standing about him, willing them to think well of his cause, and not to doubt but that his body dying in the quarrel, should rise again to life. And, said he, I doubt not but God will show you some token thereof. At length he being well nigh half burnt, and all black with fire, clustered together as in a lump like a black coal, all men thinking him dead, suddenly rose upright before the people, lifting up the stumps of his arms, and clapping the same together, declaring a rejoicing heart unto them ; and so bending down again, and hanging over the fire, slept in the Lord, and ended this mortal life.''

*Robert Smith as a writer*

To a skill in painting, Mr. Smith added one in letters, and Foxe states that '' while in prison he wrote several letters to his friends, some in verse, and others in prose ''. These poetical letters were nearly all in the same metre, part of one to a friend reading :

*Poetical Letter to a Friend*

> '' *And now because I know the goal*
>      *That thou dost most desire*
> *I send thee here a paper full,*
>      *As fined in the fire*
> *In hope thou wilt accept it well*
>      *Although it be but small*
> *Because I have no other good*
>      *To make amends withal.*'' [1]

[1] Foxe's '' Book of Martyrs.''

# The complaynt

of Veritie, made by John
Bradford.

An exhortacion of Mathewe
Rogers, vnto his children.

The complaynt of Raufe Al-
lerton and others, being priso
ners in Lolers tower, ⁊ wryt-
ten with their bloud, how god
was their comforte.

¶ A songe of Caine and Abell.

The saieng of maister Houper, that he
wrote the night before he suffered, vp-
pon a wall with a cole, in the newe In,
at Glocetet, and his saiyng
at his deathe.

ANNO DOMINI . 1559.

To his brother he also wrote, be-
speaking his care for his wife and

> " *Also my daughter dear*
> *Whom I bequeath to thee*
> *To be brought up in fear*
> *And learn the A B C*
>     *That she may grow in grace*
> *And ruled by the rod*
> *To learn and lead her life*
> *Within the fear of God.*"

*Poetical Letter
to his brother*

Far surpassing these poems in popularity, however, was the " Exhortation
vnto his children " which he penned
at this same time. Written in the
year in which he was burned (1555),
it seems to have been printed first in
1559 when the Stationers Company
directed that " Owyn Rogers hath
lycense to prynte *the Instruction for
Chyldren* ".[1] It was accordingly issued

*Writing and
publishing of
his* Exhorta-
tion unto his
children

---

[1] Arber's " Stationers' Register," 1.,96.

in that year, in a little tract of Puritan writings, on the title of which it was termed " An exhortacion of Mathewe Rogers, vnto his children ", in the body of the work it was retitled " The instruction of a Father to his Children, which he wrote a few days before his burnynge ", and at the end it was signed " Finis quod Mathewe Rogers." It apparently proved a work of some popularity for in 1577 the Stationers Company " Licensed vnto " John Arnold the issuing of another edition of the tract.

*Substitution of Rogers' Name* Why the name of Mathewe Rogers was substituted for that of the true writer can not be discovered, unless, Rogers being the earliest, and therefore the best known of the " reformed " Martyrs, the printer reasoned that his name would cause a greater sale. The change of his true cognomen John to Mathew, is more easily explained, for under the pen name of Thomas Mathew, Rogers had helped Tyndale in translating the scriptures, and thus he was often called Mathew Rogers.

But this foisting of the poem of Smith on to Rogers by no means ended the garbling. In the New England Primer, a short sketch of Rogers was inserted, as follows :

New England Primer *account of John Rogers*

" Mr. John Rogers, Minister of the Gospel in London, was the First Martyr in Queen Mary's Reign, and was burnt in Smithfield, February the 14th, 1554. His Wife with nine small Children, and one at her Breast, follow'd him to the Stake, with which sorrowful Sight, he was not in the least daunted, but with wonderful Patience,

Dyed couragiously for the Gospel of Jesus Christ."

*True account of John Rogers*

This is more remarkable for misstatement than for fact. Rogers was a priest sworn to celibacy, who becoming converted, broke his vow and took unto himself a wife. When, on the accession of Mary, he refused to put the woman away, he was condemned to death, and was burned at the stake on February 4th, 1555, "old style" February the 14, 1554 being, as Foxe said "the first martyr of all the blessed company that suffered in Queen Mary's time, that gave the first adventure upon the fire".[1]   Furthermore, his wife and children did not see him burned, for Foxe merely stated that : "His wife and children, being

[1] Foxe's "Book of Martyrs."

eleven in number, ten able to go, and one sucking at her breast, met him by the way as he went towards Smithfield: this sorrowful sight of his own flesh and blood could nothing move him, but he constantly and cheerfully took his death with wonderful patience, in the defence of the gospel of Christ".

Worth noting in this connection is one question over which there has *The number* been much controversy, being the *of John* exact number of children thus left *Rogers'* fatherless. The Primer, as will be *children* seen, gave him " nine small children and one at the breast " but printers read this differently, sometimes giving nine, and sometimes ten, in the picture. At his trial, Rogers said distinctly that he had ten children, while Foxe [1] speaks

[1] Foxe's " Book of Martyrs."

of his " children, being eleven in number, ten able to go, and one sucking ". The explanation of this discrepancy is probably due to the fact that Rogers was held in prison for over a year, and debarred during that period from all news of his wife, in which time it is obvious the eleventh child was born, since at the time of his burning it was still unweaned.

\* \* \*

*The Cate-chisms of the New England Primer*

OF greater importance than the Roger verses but of far less popularity was the Catechism, which usually followed close upon the poem. In all eighteenth century Primers examined this consisted of either the Westminster Assembly's

The *SHORTER*

# CATECHISM

*Compos'd by the*

REVEREND ASSEMBLY of

# DIVINES

At *WESTMINSTER.*

*With Proofs thereof out of the Scriptures*

Which are either some of the formerly quoted places, or others gathered
from their other Writings; all fitted
both for Brevity & Clearness, to this
their *Form of Sound Words.*

For the Benefit of Christians in ge-
*neral, and of Youth & Children in un-*
*derstanding in particular; that they*
*may with more ease acquaint them-*
*selves with the Truth according to the*
*Scriptures, and with the Scriptures*
*themselves.*

Printed by *B. Harris,* and *J. Allen,*
and are to be Sold at the *London-*
*Coffee House.* 1691

" Shorter Catechism " or John Cotton's " Spiritual Milk for Babes " and
in a number of editions both were included. Several nineteenth century
editions of the New England Primer
contained besides the Assembly's Catechism, the Episcopal as well, but no
early edition found contains what was
so alien to all the rest of the work.

The Shorter Catechism — " that
Golden Composure," as Cotton
Mather termed it — was framed by
the great Westminster Assembly,
which was called together by the
Round-Head Parliament and was composed of one hundred and twenty-one
clergymen or presbyters, thirty of the
laity, chiefly of the nobility, and five
special commissioners from Scotland,
and Baxter claimed " that the Chris-

*History of the
Shorter Cate-
chism*

tian world, since the days of the
Apostles, never had a Synod of more
excellent divines". This assembly
met first on July 10, 1643, and dis-
solved itself on March 3, 1649, having held in the six years no less
than eleven hundred and sixty-three
sessions.

*Length and consequent loathing*

Compared to Herbert's catechism
entitled "The Careful Father and
Pious Child" (London, 1648) which
contained over twelve hundred questions and answers, the assembly's catechism might well be termed "shorter".
As a fact however this title was given
merely to distinguish it from the larger
catechism put forth by this Assembly,
and its one hundred and seven questions, the answers to which ranged in
length from eight to one hundred

words, made it a nightmare to children. Nor did the elders fail to realize its terrors. Livermore found in a New England court record, a penalty imposed on an apple stealing youngster, that he was to choose whether he would be imprisoned for a stated time, or before the Saturday night ensuing learn and repeat to the magistrate the whole of the catechism. Rev. Heman Humphreys, though a Congregational clergyman and the president of Amherst College, acknowledged that his recollection " accords with the experience of thousands, who like myself, once loathed the Assembly's Catechism ",[1] and when it is considered that children of four and five years of age were expected to repeat, with

[1] " New England Primer," Worcester: [1850?]

6

absolute verbal correctness, the terrible
answers defining "justification",
"sanctification", and "glorification",
or stand disgraced in the eyes of the
whole congregation, the word seems
by no means too strong. Another clergyman acknowledged that "when the
Venerable Assembly composed this
form of Instruction, it seems that
few of themselves tho't it design'd or
fitted for Babes, some answers being
so long and so full of great sense that
tho' they might recite the Words, that
can be of little Benefit, till they also
apprehend the meaning".[1]

None the less the children were
drilled in this catechism unsparingly.
In church and at school it was almost

*A daily task for Children*

[1] Noble's "Beginners' Catechism." London:
1707.

a daily task. As if this were not sufficient Cotton Mather even advised mothers to catechise their children "every day," adding "you may be continually dropping something of the *Catechism* upon them : Some *Honey out of the Rock!*" and he told parents that :

"The *Souls* of your *Children* made a Cry in your Ears, O *Parents*; a cry enough to break an Heart of Adamant. They are *Born Children of Wrath*; and when they grow up, you have no way to *Save* them from the dreadful *Wrath* of God, if you do not *Catechise* them in the *Way of Salvation*. They cry to you ; O *our dear Parents*; *Acquaint us with the Great God, and His Glorious Christ, that so Good may come unto us! Let us not go from your Tender Knees, down to the Place of Dragons.* Oh! Not *Parents*, but *Ostriches*: Not *Parents*, but *Prodigies!* What, but more cruel than

*Mr. Cotton Mather : his views on Catechising*

the *Sea-Monsters* are the *Parents*, who will
not be moved by such Thoughts as these,
to *Draw out the Breasts* of the *Catechism*,
unto their *Young Ones!* One would think,
*Parents*, Your own *Bowels*, if you have
not *Monstrously* lost them, would Suggest
enough to persuade you unto the *Pleasant
Labours* of the *Catechism*."

Yet even Mather acknowledged that the
Shorter Catechism had difficulties for
very young children, by preparing a
briefer and simpler one, that instead of
taxing children of the " Youngest and
Lowest Capacities," with the catechism
of the Assembly, "This little *Watering
Pot* may be quickly so used upon the
little Olive Plants about our tables, that,
not a drop of the heavenly dew contained in it shall escape them ".[1]

[1] " Man of God Furnished:" 1708.

Nor was the catechism used only for the catechising of the younger generation, for it was frequently made the subject of sermons to the elder portions of the congregation, Mather relating that Rev. John Fiske "chose the Assembly's Catechism for his public expositions, wherewith he twice went over it, in his discourses before his afternoon sermons." The largest book printed in New England before the nineteenth century, was Samuel Willard's "Complete Body of Divinity in Two Hundred and Fifty Expository Lectures on the Assembly's Shorter Catechism" — a mammoth folio of over nine hundred pages, of such popularity that before publication more than five hundred subscribers were obtained, many of whom bespoke

*Sermonizing on the Catechism*

more than one copy, and some as many as sixteen.

It has been questioned whether the Assembly's Catechism appeared in the very earliest editions of the New England Primer, but from the fact that Harris printed a separate edition of the catechism in the same year that the second impression of the Primer was issued, the evidence seems far more in favor of its inclusion than against it.

*Early editions of the Primer and the Catechism*

*\* \**

EQUALLY popular at first in America was John Cotton's "Spiritual Milk for American Babes," Mather being authority for the statement that in 1697 "the children of New England are to this

*Cotton's Spiritual Milk for Babes*

# MILK
## FOR
# BABES.

### DRAWN
## Out of the Breasts of both
### TESTAMENTS.

Chiefly, for the spirituall nourishment
of *Boston* Babes in either *England*:
But may be of like use for any
Children.

---

*By* JOHN COTTON, *B. D.*
*and Teacher to the Church of* Boston
*in* New-England.

---

*LONDON,*
Printed by *J. Coe,* for *Henry Overton,*
and are to be sold at his Shop, in
*Popes-head* Alley.
1646.

day most usually fed with this excellent catechism " [1] and he called it
" peculiarly, *The Catechism* of New
England."

Of the author Mather wrote:

" Were I master of the pen, wherewith
*Palladius* embalmed his *Chrysostom*, the
Greek patriark, or *Posidonius* eternized his
*Austin*, the Latin oracle, among the an-
cients ; or, were I owner of the quill
wherewith among the moderns, *Beza* cele-
brated his immortal *Calvin*, or *Fabius* im-
mortalized his venerable *Beza ;* the merits
of *John Cotton* would oblige me to employ
it, in the preserving his famous memory ".[2]

*Some Account*
*of Mr. Cotton*

It is sufficient to say that he was born
in 1585, went through Cambridge
University and became successively
fellow of Trinity College, Dean of

---

[1] Mather's " Magnalia."      [2] *Ibid.*

Emmanuel College, and minister at Boston in Lincolnshire. Becoming while there a non-conformist, he was " silenced " for a while, but eventually was allowed once more to preach, and in his twenty years pastorate at Boston " he thrice went over the *body of divinity* in a *catechistical way*, and besides his ' Lord's day ' sermons " gave " his ordinary lecture every week, on the *week days*, namely on *Wednesdays* and *Thursdays*, early in the morning, and on Saturdays, at three in the afternoon ", with such results to Boston that " religion was embraced, and practiced among the *body* of the people ; yea the *mayor*, with most part of the magistrates, were now called *Puritans*, and the *Satanical party* was become insignificant ".

Finally the High Commission Court, popularly known as the Star Chamber, began proceedings against him, and changing name and garb, Cotton took ship for New England with two other clergymen, the three lightening the tedium of the passage by daily sermons "all the while they were aboard, yea they had three sermons, or expositions, for the most part every day: of Mr. *Cotton* in the morning, Mr. *Hooker* in the afternoon, Mr. *Stone* after supper in the evening". Upon arriving at Boston he was promptly made "teacher" of the first church there, and very quickly came to wield a power in that theocratic settlement akin to that now exercised by a political boss. He was invited to return to England when the Puritans gained

*Flies to America and becomes a Leader*

the upper hand, to take part in the "Westminster Assembly" but declined. Nothing perhaps better typifies the man than when on "being asked why in his latter days he indulged in *nocturnal studies* more than formerly, he pleasantly replied, *Because I love to sweeten my mouth with a piece of* Calvin *before I go to sleep*".[1]

*Prepares Milk for Babes*

Cotton presumably prepared the Milk for Babes in 1641, at the time the "General Corte" asked the elders to prepare a catechism, as already recorded, and probably it was printed at Cambridge by Daye, between 1641 and 1645. No copy of this edition is known however, and the first edition of which a copy is now extant is one printed in London in 1646. It

[1] Mather's "Magnalia."

was again printed there in 1648 and
1668, and in 1656 an edition was issued at Cambridge in New England.
After 1690 its inclusion in many editions of the New England Primer
somewhat checked the printing of
separate issues, but an edition in the
Indian tongue was printed at Boston
in 1691, and this was reprinted in
1720. In 1702 Mather abridged and
combined it with the Assembly's catechism and one of his own and issued
it under the title of " Maschil, or The
Faithful Instructor ", and other editions of this form of the work were
issued with the title of " The Man of
God Furnished " (Boston 1708) and
" The Way of Truth laid out "
(Boston 1721). In these, Mather
asserted that Milk for Babes " will be

valued and studied and improved until New England cease to be New England."

While by no means as popular as Mr. Cotton's metaphorical title would lead one to expect, it must be confessed that it is a decided improvement on the Shorter Catechism, if not in soundness of doctrine, at least in length. In place of one hundred and seven questions, there were but sixty-four and instead of replies ranging in length from eight to one hundred words, one answer was a single word, and the longest only contained eighty-four.

Milk for Babes *compared with the* Shorter Catechism

\* \*
\*

THE last piece of any importance which can be considered an integrant of the New England Primer, is what was called "A Dialogue between Christ, Youth and the Devil", a poem relating to a tempted youth, who despite the warning of his Redeemer succumbs to the wiles of the horny footed tempter, and makes an effective exit at the end of the dialogue without the assistance of any stage directions, but with, it is presumable, the glare of subterranean regions, in place of the more professional calcium light.

*Dialogue between Christ, Youth and the Devil*

This dialogue form was a favorite medium of the seventeenth century. In 1671 Thomas Sherman issued a tract called "Youth's Tragedy, drawn up by way of Dialogue between Youth,

*Popularity of Dialogue form*

the Devil, Wisdom, Time, Death, the Soul, and the Nuncius", which was many times reprinted. So too, an anonymous poem entitled " An Excellent Example to all young Men, being a Dialogue betwixt Youth and Conscience and Satan" was issued in London in 1684. Still a third, called " The Youth's Looking Glass, being a divine Dialogue between a young Man, Satan, and our Saviour Jesus Christ", was printed without a date.

*Authorship of Dialogue*

None of these were the same as the Dialogue used in the Primer, and as no printing of it can be found pre-dating its appearance in that publication, it seems probable that it was composed by the man whom Dunton described as " the neat and poetical Ben Harris ". It is proper to note that unlike the portions already described it was not always included in the New England Primer, but as it is contained in the Bradford fragment, and in Harris' " New English Tutor ", as well as in nine editions of the Primer printed in the eighteenth century, it has seemed best to treat it as one of the true pieces that went to mark the little book.

*<sub>*</sub>*

SUCH were the main contents of the Primer, but many smaller pieces, in which far greater variation was shown, were used by the printers to fill in between the more important portions, and to pad out at the end so as to complete the last signature. Few of these minor pieces

*Minor Varia-tions in the Primer*

can be positively identified, but as they go to make a history of the book, and as their chronology is of some value in settling the approximate decade of imperfect copies of the Primer, they deserve some attention.

*Prayer of Edward VIth*

In the second edition of the Primer, as the advertisement states, the Prayer of Edward VI, taken from Foxe's "Book of Martyrs" was given, and this prayer appears in the "New English Tutor", but no Primer extant contains it.

*Text of Earliest Editions*

The New English Tutor, The Protestant Tutors of 1715, and 1716, and the New England Primer of 1727 contain the ten commandments, the "Names and Orders of the Books of the Old and New Testament" and "Numeral Letters and Figures, which may serve for the ready finding of any Chapter and Verse in the Bible". None of these were included in the later eighteenth century editions.

In the edition of 1737 a longish "Verses for Children" beginning "Though I am but a little one" appeared for the first time, and was included in many subsequent editions. This edition also gave a part of the "Duty of Children towards their Parents" which had been given in the "New English Tutor". The only other edition with this was one printed in London in 1781. Most remarkable of all in this edition was its printing of the lines:

*Text of edition of 1737*

> " *Now I lay me down to sleep*
> *I pray the Lord my soul to keep*
> *If I should die before I wake*
> *I pray the Lord my soul to take.*"

7

The author of these famous lines is unknown, and this is their first appearance in print, so far as can be discovered. They were included in almost every subsequent edition of the Primer.

*Text of the Evangelized Editions*

With the evangelization of the Primer between 1740 and 1760, besides the change in the rhymed alphabet other material alterations were introduced. In the earliest edition extant so revised the chief variations are the introduction of Watts' Divine Song for Children, his Cradle Hymn, and his Morning and Evening Prayers, Rev. Nathaniel Clap's " Advice to his Children," " Agurs Prayer," (which had appeared in the " New English Tutor ") and " Some Proper Names of Men and Women." All

these additions proved fairly popular,
though the parts by Watts were the
most so, and they formed the text of
most editions of the Primer issued
between 1762 and 1790. A minor
addition was the insertion of a short
set of questions, beginning " Who was
the first Man ", and all to be answered
from the Bible. This was lengthened
or shortened at the will of each
printer, and in the Salem edition of
1784 the printer so far departed
from sacred text, as to ask " Who
saved America " and " Who betrayed
America," the answers being " George
Washington " and " Benedict Arnold."

About 1790 a very marked change
was made by printers taking some mundane rhymes from an English publication entitled the " Royal Primer ",

describing various animals, with pictures of them. From this source were also taken a " Description of a Good Boy ", a " Description of a Bad Boy," and poems on " The Good Girl " and " The Naughty Girl ". Their insertion marked the beginning of the end, for no longer salvation was promised to the good, and unending fire to the bad, but " pert Miss Prat-a-pace " was to have none of the " Orange, Apples, Cakes, or Nuts " promised to " pretty Miss Prudence," and the naughty urchin was only threatened with beggary while the good boy was promised " credit and reputation ". Worst of all was the insertion of a short poem which should have made the true Puritan turn in his grave, for instead of teaching that let-

Cuts of Animals

(From the "New England Primer." Newburyport [N. D.])

For ever will a blockhead be:

| N Nag | O Owl | P Peacock |
| Q Queen | R Robin | S Squirrel |
| T Top | V Vine | W Whale |
| X Xerxes | Y Young Lamb | Z Zany |

B

ters were to be learned, that the Bible
might be read, and that the figures
were to be acquired for the purpose of
finding chapter and verse in that work,
it said:

> " *He who ne'er learns his A. B. C.*
> *Forever will a blockhead be.*
> *But he who learns his letters fair*
> *Shall have a coach to take the air.*"

The change, nevertheless proved popular, alas, and quite a number of
editions between 1790 and 1800 contain
more or less of these worldly additions.

Of these successive variations in the
American primer, British editions took
no heed, and they constitute a class by
themselves. Although Harris' issue
of the Primer in Old England contained Cotton's " Milk for Babes,"
later English editions did not include

*Unvarying-
ness of Eng-
lish Editions*

it. But aside from the standard contents of the Primer, there were added " The History of the Creation," a poetical " Advice to Children," a " Collection of the best English Proverbs," and a number of shorter pieces.

*
* *

*The " Adornment " with Cuts*

NO account of the Primer would be complete without some notice of the illustrations, which alone of all its contents bid for popular favor from the children. In the Protestant Tutor as printed by Harris in 1679, is a frontispiece typemetal cut of Charles I. and from the fact that the New English Tutor and the 1727 edition of the Primer both lack the preliminary leaf of the first

Portrait of Charles II

(From the " Protestant Tutor."   London : 16-9)

King *GEORGE* the Third,
Crown'd *September* 22d 1761,

(From the " New England Primer."   Boston : 1762)

KING *GEORGE* ... ...
crowned *September* ... 1751.

signature it is a safe assumption that these two books each began with a portrait of the Royal personage reigning at the time of their issue. The Protestant Tutor of 1716 has a cut of George I. The Primer of 1737 gives a very fairly executed portrait of George II. In 1762, though news of the death of this monarch had reached Boston, yet in an edition of the book printed there in that year, there either was too little time, or the printer was too economical, to prepare a new cut, so an additional stroke of the burin changed a II. into a III., and thus a portrait of George III. was improvised, which in its striking likeness to his father clearly shows the wonderful influence of heredity.

The Primer of 1770 was more his-

*The English King.*

torically correct, giving a genuine though very crude portrait of George III. Again however, the printer was called upon, by the American Revolution, to change his frontispiece, and in 1776 the portrait of the Royal George was merely relabelled, and came forth as the republican " John Hancock ", the likeness between these two being, it is needless to say, very extraordinary considering that they were representatives of such opposite parties. In the Boston edition of 1777 a correct portrait of Hancock was achieved, and in an edition printed in Hartford in the same year a portrait of Samuel Adams, another hero of the hour, was given. At the end of the revolution, the standard portrait became that of Washington, and the

(From the " American Primer."   Boston : 1776)

# THE Hon. SAMUEL ADAMS *Esquire.*

(From the " New England Primer." Hartford: 1---)

only exception to the use of his features, when any portrait was given in subsequent editions, is one of Isaac Watts printed in a Worcester edition issued about 1850.

The changes in the rhymed alphabet cuts have already been described. One important fact however, is the use of some of the little pictures in a work written by Harris entitled " The Holy Bible In Verse." Harris advertised this book as early as 1701, and in an edition printed in 1717 all of the cuts are clearly taken from his edition of the New England Primer.

*The Rhymed Alphabet Cuts*

The print of John Rogers at the stake has also been mentioned. There is a picture of the scene in Foxe's " Book of Martyrs," but this departs from the standard of the Primer cuts,

*The Prints of John Rogers*

by not having wife and children present. The earliest cut found to include them is contained in the " New English Tutor," and the identical block used in that work is also used in Harris' edition of the " Protestant Tutor " of 1715. Probably the most curious of all is that contained in the Albany edition of 1818, in which the guards are costumed in the local militia uniform of the day, with great plumes in their shakos, but scarcely less odd is that in the Lansingburg, 1810 edition, in which the executioner is given a continental cocked hat.

*The Pope, or Man of Sin*

In the " New English Tutor " a print is given of " The Pope or Man of Sin " which was originally beyond question a cut used to illustrate the signs of the zodiac in an almanac, for

## The POPE, or Man of Sin:

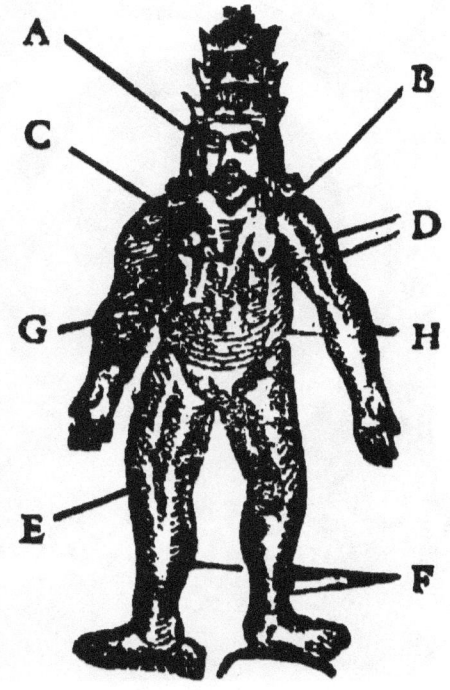

(From the " New English Tutor."　London : [1702–1714?])

Queen, 1737

(From the " New England Primer."   Boston : 1737)

it is exactly like them with the exception of the addition of a tiara to the otherwise naked figure. To utilize the zodiacal lines and letters radiating from the body, Harris added a key or explanation which replaced Aries, Taurus, Cancer, Scorpion, etc., with Heresy, Disorder, Malice, Murder and Treachery, etc., and which called on the " Child " to " behold that Man of Sin, the Pope, worthy thy utmost Hatred." This print was reproduced in the Primer of 1737, but no key was added, so that the " Child " must have been not a little puzzled to know what the rays and letters meant.

There was a worse lapse, however, in this edition of 1737, for the last leaf prints an engraving which certainly was nothing less than the block

*The Devil's Picture Card*

of the queen in playing cards, for contemporary packs have just such queens. To find such a print in the godly New England Primer is perhaps the most curious fact yet known, and can only be accounted for by the probability that its purchasers were so ignorant of the appearance of the " Devil's picture cards " that they did not recognize its prototype.

*Biblical and Worldly Illustrations*

The " New English Tutor " contained pictures of Death, Judgment, Heaven, and Hell, but these do not seem to have been repeated in the Primer. Kindred illustrations however, of " Adam and Eve ", the " Nativity and the Passion ", " Christ's Death ", and " The Ascension " were given in the Salem edition of 1784, and some of these prints were used

**On Death**

*View, my dear Child, what is before thine Eye.*
*And know for certain thou art born to dye*
*How soon thou know'st not, it may come before:*
*Thou shalt enjoy one Minutes Pleasure more ;*
*When thou wilt leave this World and all behind,*
*To be with Worms, in some Church, yard confind.*
*And as from all thy friends grim death shall take thee*
*So God will find thee when the trumpet shall awake*

(From the "New English Tutor."   London : 1702-1714?])

in other issues printed in the decade
1790–1800. This Salem edition contained pictures of "a little boy and
girl bestowing charity" and "a good
Boy and Girl at their Books." More
important still was its inclusion of
certain prints of animals taken from
the "Royal Primer," which, with the
already described poems, was the first
true bid for popularity the Primer had
ever made. Some other worldly prints
were included, among them two designed to teach the alphabet, no longer
by Bible extracts, but by pictures of
playthings, animals, etc.

This secularizing was an attack by
its friends from which the book never
quite recovered, for the printers having
once found how much more saleable
such primers were, and parents having

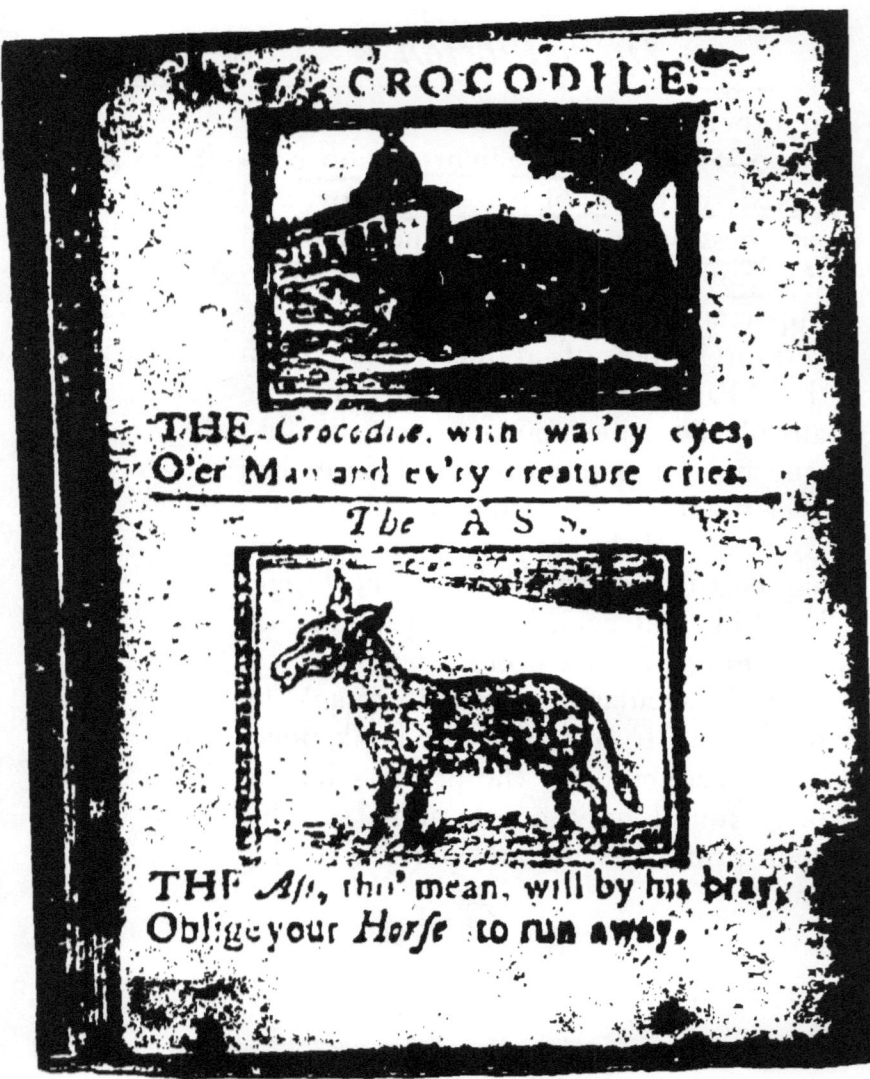

THE *Crocodile*, with wat'ry eyes,
O'er Man and ev'ry creature cries.

The ASS.

THE *Ass*, tho' mean, will by his bray,
Oblige your *Horse* to run away.

(From the " New England Primer." Newburyport [N. D.])

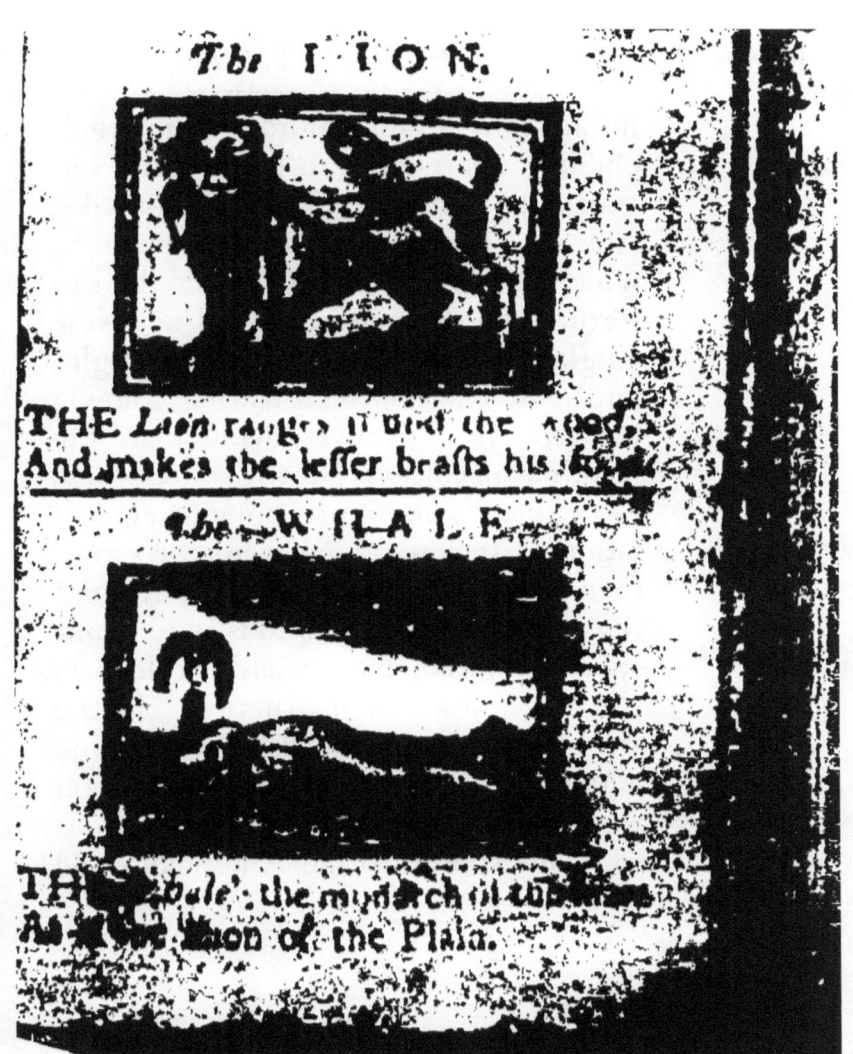

## The LION.

THE Lion ranges o'er the wood,
And makes the lesser beasts his food.

## the WHALE

THE Whale: the monarch of the main,
As is the Lion of the Plain.

(From the "New England Primer." Newburyport [N. D.])

found how much more readily their
children learned, both united in en-
couraging more popular school-books,
and very quickly illustrated primers,
which aimed to please rather than to
torture, were multiplied. The New
England Primer made a brave fight,
but it was a hopeless battle. Slowly
printer after printer abandoned the
printing of editions of the little work,
in favor of some more popular compi-
lation. It was driven from the cities,
then from the villages, and finally from
the farm houses. Editions were constantly printed, but steadily it lost its
place as a book of instruction. In the
schools it was replaced by other and
better books, and though an edition
was printed as recently as 1886, it is
to be questioned if an American child

of to-day is being taught by the famous
little manual.

\*
\* \*

IT is impossible to measure the
work the Primer accomplished. *The Work of*
If the Puritan exodus is viewed *the Primer*
with the eyes of the Hon. William
Stoughton, who asserted that " God
sifted a whole nation that he might
send choice grain into this wilder-
ness," there was little left for the
Primer to do. This however is a
public speaker's view, and therefore
probably approximated more to what
would please his audience, than to the
truth. Certainly the court records of
early New England reveal a condition
akin to all frontier settlements in law-
lessness and immorality, and in pro-

portion to population show a greater percentage of most crimes than would be found even in our large cities of to-day, bearing out the statement of the Rev. John White, — a leading Puritan — that a large part of the first settlers of New England were "a multitude of rude ungovernable persons, the very scum of the land." It is related that a newly installed New England pastor said to a spinster parishioner "I hope, madam, you believe in total depravity," and received the prompt response: "Oh, parson, what a fine doctrine it would be, if folks only lived up to it." There was far more living up to total depravity in early New England than most people suspect, and when one reads the charges brought against them by

their own ministers, it is not difficult
to realize why the New England
clergy dwelt so much on the terrors
of hell; one even becomes sympathetic
with the Presbyterian clergyman who
said with disgust that "the Universal-
ists believe that all men will be saved,
but we hope for better things." What-
ever the first years of New England
may have been, however, the church
and the school were at work, and what
they did needs no other monument
than the history of the last two hundred years. The New England Primer
is dead, but it died on a victorious
battle field, and its epitaph may well
be that written of Noah Webster's
Spelling Book:

"It taught millions to read, and not
one to sin."

8

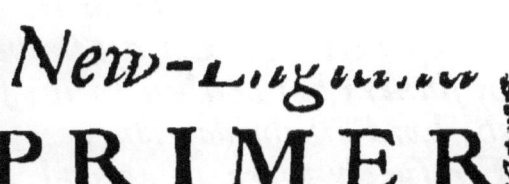

# PRIMER

Enlarged.

For the more eaſy attaining
the true Reading of ENGLISH

To which is added,

The Aſſembly of Divines

# *CATECHISM.*

---

*BOSTON:* Printed by *S Kneeland,* &
*T. Green,* Sold by the Bookſellers. 1727

.ue. will not depart from it.

Chap. 23. 17; 18. Let not thy heart
envy sinners, but be thou in the fear
of the Lord all the day long.

For surely there is an end, and
thy expectation shall not be cut off.

Eph. 1. 1. Children obey your Parents in the Lord, for this is right.

Of Serving GOD.

1. God will have no time to save
us, if we find no day to serve Him.

2. Shall we have six days in
seven, and God not one?

1 Chron. 28. 9. My son, know thou
the God of thy Father, & serve Him with
a perfect heart, & with a willing mind,
for the Lord searcheth all hearts.

a b c d e f g h i j k l m
n o p q r s t v u w x
y z &

Vowels.

A E I O U Y    a e i o u y

Confonants,

b c d f g h i k f m n p q r f t v w x z

Double Letters,

Italick Letters.

Aa Bb Cc Dd Ee Ff Gg Hh
Ii Kk Ll Mm Nn Oo Pp Qq
Rr Sf Tt Uu Ww Xx Yy Zz

Italick Double Letters

## The Great English Letters,

A B C D E F G H I
K L M N O P Q R
S T U W X Y Z.

## The Small English Letters.

a b c d e f g h i k l m n o
p q r z ſ s t u w x y z &.

## Great Letters.

A B C D E F G H I K L M N O
P Q R S T U V W X Y Z.

### *Eaſie Syllables for Children.*

| ab | eb | ib | ob | ub |
|----|----|----|----|----|
| ac | ec | ic | oc | uc |
| ad | ed | id | od | ud |
| af | ef | if | of | uf |
| ag | eg | ig | og | ug |
| ak | ek | ik | ok | uk |
| al | el | il | ol | ul |

| | | | | |
|---|---|---|---|---|
| am | em | im | om | um |
| an | en | in | on | un |
| ap | ep | ip | op | up |
| ar | er | ir | or | ur |
| as | es | is | os | us |
| at | et | it | ot | ut |
| ax | ex | ix | ox | ux |
| ba | be | bi | bo | bu |
| ca | ce | ci | co | cu |
| da | de | di | do | du |
| fa | fe | fi | fo | fu |
| ga | ge | gi | go | gu |
| ha | he | hi | ho | hu |
| ka | ke | ki | ko | ku |
| la | le | li | lo | lu |
| ma | me | mi | mo | mu |
| na | ne | ni | no | nu |
| pa | pe | pi | po | pu |
| ra | re | ri | ro | ru |
| ſa | ſe | ſi | ſo | ſu |

ta     te     ti     to     tu

*Words of one Syllable.*

| | | | |
|---|---|---|---|
| Are | be | child | face |
| air | beſt | clay | fine |
| add | hed | cry | fair |
| all | hold | cup | few |
| ape | bad | ear | fight |
| God | kid | grace | give |
| great | kind | heart | hat |
| grant | kill | had | hath |
| good | kick | gooſe | glaſs |
| graſs | kiſs | hair | he |
| grew | knee | head | health |
| heal | long | nine | peace |
| how | man | no | peep |
| hide | maid | noſe | pence |
| knit | mole | of | pitch |
| known | moon | old | play |
| knew | more | once | pure |

## Words of two Syllables.

| | |
|---|---|
| Ab-ſent | Abſent |
| Bold-ly | Boldly |
| Con-ſtant | Conſtant |
| De-pend | Depend |
| En-cloſe | Encloſe |
| Fa-ther | Father |
| Glo-ry | Glory |
| Hus-band | Husband |

## Words of three Syllables.

| | |
|---|---|
| A-bu-ſing | Abuſing |
| Be-witch-ing | Bewitching |
| Con-found-ed | Confounded |
| Drun-ken-neſs | Drunkenneſs |
| E-raſ-mus | Eraſmus |
| Fa-cul-ty | Faculty |
| God-li-neſs | Godlineſs |
| Ho-li-neſs | Holineſs |
| Im-pu-dent | Impudent |
| Ka-len-der | Kalender. |

## Words of four Syllables.

| | |
|---|---|
| Ac·com pa·ny | Accompany |
| Be·ne·vo·lence | Benevolence |
| Ce·re·mo·ny | Ceremony |
| Dif·con·tent·ed | Difcontented |
| E·ver·laft·ing | Everlafting |
| Fi·de·li·ty | Fidelity |
| Glo·ri·fy·ing | Glorifying |
| Hu·mi·li·ty | Humility |
| In·fir·mi·ty | Infirmity. |

## Words of five Syllables.

| | |
|---|---|
| Ad mi·ra·ti·on | Admiration |
| Be·ne·fi·ci al | Beneficial |
| Con·fo·la ti·on | Confolation |
| De cla ra ti·on | Declaration |
| Ex hor·ta·ti·on | Exhortation |
| For·ni·ca·ti on | Fornication |
| Ge·ne·ra ti·on | Generation |
| Ha·bi'ta·ti·on | Habitation |
| In·vi·ta ti on | Invitation |

A    In *Adam's* Fall
We Sinned all.

B    Thy Life to Mend
This *Book* Attend.

C    The *Cat* doth play
And after flay.

D    A *Dog* will bite
A Thief at night.

E    An *Eagles* flight
Is out of fight.

F    The Idle *Fool*
Is whipt at School.

G    As runs the *Glaſs*
Mans life doth paſs.

H    My *Book* and *Heart*
Shall never part.

J    *Job* feels the Rod
Yet bleſſes GOD.

K    Our *K I N G* the good
No man of blood.

L    The *Lion* bold
The *Lamb* doth hold.

M    The *Moon* gives light
In time of night.

**N**    *Nightingales* sing
In Time of Spring.

**O**    The *Royal Oak*
it was the Tree
That sav'd His
Royal Majeſtie.

**P**    *Peter* denies
His Lord and cries.

**Q**    Queen *Eſther* comes
in Royal State
To Save the JEWS
from diſmal Fate

**R**    *Rachel* doth mour.
For her firſt born.

**S**    *Samuel* anoints
Whom God appoint:

**T** Time cuts down all
Both great and small.

**U** Uriah's beauteous Wife
Made *David* feek his
Life.

**W** Whales in the Sea
God's Voice obey.

**X** Xerxes the great did
die,
And fo mult you & I.

**Y** Youth forward flips
Death fooneft nips.

**Z** Zacheus he
Did climb the Tree
His Lord to fee,

*Now the Child being entred in his Letters and Spelling, let him learn these and such like Sentences by Heart, whereby he will be both instructed in his Duty, and encouraged in his Learning.*

### The Dutiful Child's Promises,

I Will fear GOD, and honour the KING.
   I will honour my Father & Mother.
I will Obey my Superiours.
I will Submit to my Elders,
I will Love my Friends.
I will hate no Man.
I will forgive my Enemies, and pray to
         God for them.
I will as much as in me lies keen all God's
         Holy Commandments.

I will learn my Catechism.
I will keep the Lord's Day Holy.
I will Reverence God's Sanctuary,
  For our GOD is a consuming Fire.

*An Alphabet of Lessons for Youth.*

**A** Wise Son makes a glad Father, but a foolish Son is the heaviness of his Mother.

**B** Etter is a little with the fear of the Lord, than great treasure and trouble therewith.

**C** Ome unto CHRIST all ye that labour and are heavy laden, and He will give you rest.

**D** O not the abominable thing which I hate, faith the Lord.

**E** Xcept a Man be born again, he cannot see the Kingdom of God.

**F** Oolishness is bound up in the heart of a Child, but the rod of Correction shall drive it far from him.

**G** Rieve not the Holy Spirit.

**H**Olineſs becomes God's Houſe for
ever.

**I**T is good for me to draw near unto
God.

**K**Eep thy Heart with all Diligence, for
out of it are the iſſues of Life.

**L**iars ſhall have their part in the lake
which burns with fire and brimſtone.

**M**Any are the Afflictions of the
Righteous, but the Lord delivers
them out of them all.

**N**OW is the accepted time, now is
the day of ſalvation.

**O**Ut of the abundance of the heart
the mouth ſpeaketh.

**P**Ray to thy Father which is in ſecret,
and thy Father which ſees in ſecret,
ſhall reward thee openly.

**Q**Uit you like Men, be ſtrong, ſtand
faſt in the Faith.

**R**Emember thy Creator in the days
of thy Youth.

**S**Alvation belongeth to the Lord.

TRust in God at all times ye peopl. pour out your hearts before him.

UPon the wicked God shall rain an horrible Tempest.

WO to the wicked, it shall be ill with him, for the reward of his hands shall be given him.

EXHort one another daily while Is is called to day, left any of you be hardened through the deceitfulness of Sin.

YOung Men ye have overcome the wicked one.

ZEal hath confumed me, because thy enemies have forgotten the words of God.          *Choice Sentences.*

1. Praying will make thee leave fin ning, or finning will make thee leave praying.

2. Our Weaknefs and Inabilities break not the bond of our Duties.

3. What we are afraid to fpeak before Men, we fhould be afraid to think before Cod.

The

## The LORD's Prayer.

OUR Fa·ther which art in Hea·ven, Hal·low·ed be thy Name. Thy King·dom come. Thy Will be done on Earth as it is in Hea·ven. Give us this day our dai·ly Bread. And for·give us our Debts as we for·give our Deb·tors. And lead us not in·to Temp·ta·ti·on, but de·li·ver us from e·vil, for thine is the Kingdom, the Pow·er and the Glo·ry, for e·ver, A·MEN.

## The CREED.

I Be·lieve in GOD the Fa·ther Almigh·ty, Ma·ker of Hea·ven and Earth. And in Je·sus Chrilt his on·ly Son our Lord, which was con·ceiv·ed by the Ho·ly Ghoft, Born of the Vir·gin *Mary*, Suf·fer·ed un·der *Pon·ti·us Pi·late*, was cru·ci·fi·ed, Dead and Bu·ri·ed, He de·fcen·ded in·to Hell. The third Day he·a·rofe a·gain from the Dead ; and af·fcen·ded in·to Hea·ven, and fit·teth on the Right Hand of God the Fa·ther Al·migh·ty From thence he fhall come to judg·es the quick and the dead. I be-lieve in the Ho-ly Ghoft, the Ho-ly Ca-tho-lick Church, the Com-mu-ni-on of Saints, the For-give-nefs of Sins, the Re-fur-rec-ti-on of the Bo-dy, and the Life E-ver-laff-ing A-MEN.

*The Ten Commandments.* Exod. XX.

GOD *fpake all thefe Words. faying,* I *am the Lord thy God, which have* brought *thee out of the Land of Ægypt, out of the Houfe of Bondage.*

I. Thou fhalt have no other gods before me.

II. Thou fhalt not make unto thee any graven Image, or any likenefs of any thing that is in Heaven above, or that is in the Earth beneath, or that is in the Water under the Earth ; thou fhalt not bow down thy felf to them, nor ferve them, for I the Lord thy God am a jea-us God, vifiting the iniquity of the Fa-iersupon the Children, unto the third

and fourth
me, and the
of them th
mandment

   III. Th
the Lo
will ne
Name

   IV
it ho,
all the
Sabbai
fhalt ne
nor thy
nor thy
the Stra
in fix
Eart
reft
ble

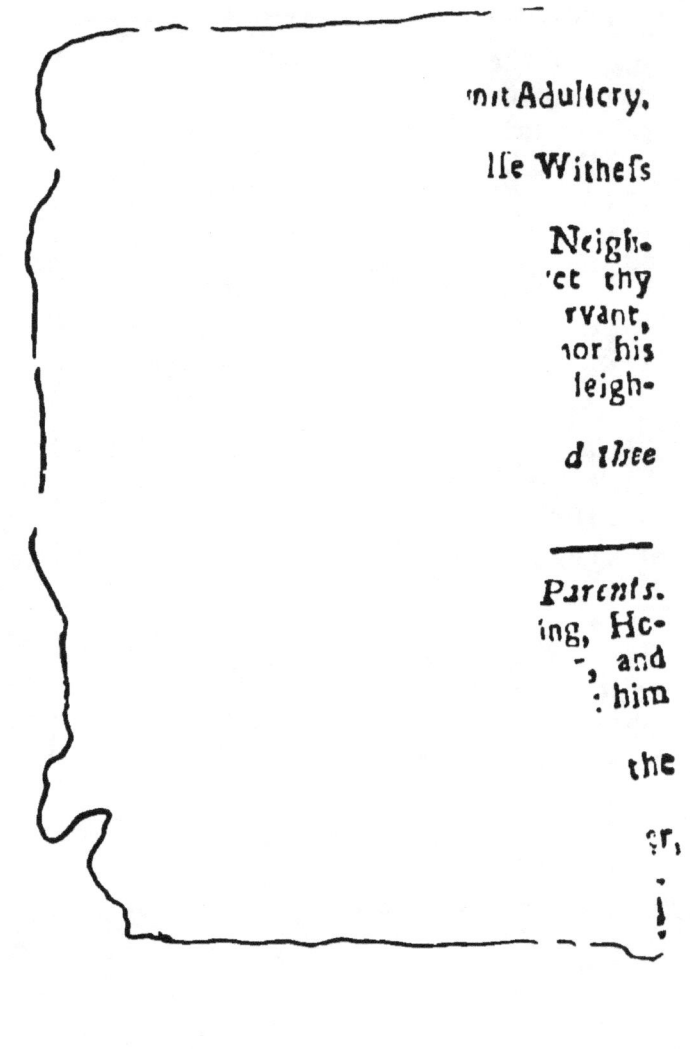

mit Adultery,

lfe Witnefs

Neigh-
et thy
rvant,
nor his
leigh-

d thee

---

Parents.
ing, He-
, and
: him

the

er,

j

and fourth Generation of them that hate me and fhewing Mercy unto thoufands of them that love Me and keep my Commandments.

III. Thou fhalt not take the Name of the Lord thy God in vain, for the Lord will not hold him guiltlefs that taketh his Name in vain.

IV. Remember the Sabbath Day and keep it holy, fix Days fhalt thou labor and do all thy Work, but the feventh day is the Sabbath of the Lord thy God, in it thou fhalt not do any work, thou nor thy Son, nor thy Daughter, nor thy Man Servant, nor thy Maid Servant, nor thy Cattle, nor the Stranger that is within thy Gates, for in fix Days the Lord made Heaven and Earth, the Sea, and all that in them is, and refted the feventh Day, wherefore the Lord blefsed the Sabbath Day and hallowed it.

V. Honor thy Father and thy Mother, that thy Days may be long upon the Land which the Lord thy God giveth thee.

VI. Thou fhalt not Kill.

*[Restoration of lacking text]*

19

VII. Thou shalt not commit Adultery.

VIII. Thou shalt not Steal.

IX. Thou shalt not bear false Witnefs againft thy Neighbor.

X. Thou shalt not covet thy Neighbor's Houfe, thou shalt not covet thy Neighbor's Wife, nor his Man Servant, nor his Maid Servant, nor his Ox, nor his Afs, nor anything that is thy Neighbor's.

*These Words which I command thee this Day shall be in thy Heart.*

### DUTY OF CHILDREN TOWARDS THEIR PARENTS.

God hath commanded faying, Honour thy Father and Mother, and whofo curfeth Father or Mother, let him die the Death. Mat. 15. 4.

Children obey your Parents in the Lord, for this is right.

2. Honour thy Father and Mother, (which is the firft Commandment with Promife).

*[Restoration of lacking text]*

3. That it may be well with thee, and that thou mayſt live long on the Earth.

Children, obey your Parents in all Things, for that is well pleaſing unto the Lord. Col. 3, 20.

The Eye that mocketh his Father, and deſpiſeth the Inſtruction of his Mother, let the Ravens of the Valley pluck it out, and the young Eagles eat it.

Father, I have ſinned againſt Heaven, and before thee. Luke 15, 10.

19. I am no more worthy to be called thy Son.

No man ever hated his own fleſh, but nouriſheth and cheriſheth it. Ephes. 5, 19.

I pray thee let my Father and Mother come and abide with you, till I know what God will do for me. 1 Sam. 22, 3.

My Son, help thy Father in his Age, and grieve him not as long as he liveth.

*[Restoration of lacking text]*

12. And if his Understanding fail, have patience with him, and despise him not when thou art in thy full Strength.

Whoso curseth his Father or his Mother, his Lamp shall be put out in obscure Darkness. Prov. 20, 20.

## VERSES.

I in the Burying Place may see
   Graves shorter there than I;
From Death's Arrest no Age is free,
   Young Children too may die;
My God, may such an awful Sight,
   Awakening be to me!
Oh! that by early Grace I might
   For Death prepared be.

## AGAIN.

First in the Morning when thou dost
   awake,
To God for his Grace thy Petition make,
Some Heavenly Petition use daily to say,
That the God of Heaven may bless
   thee alway.

*[Restoration of lacking text]*

*Good Children must,*

| | |
|---|---|
| *Fear God all Day,* | *Love Christ alway,* |
| *Parents obey,* | *In Secret Pray,* |
| *No false thing say,* | *Mind little Play,* |
| *By no Sin stray,* | *Make no delay,* |

*In doing Good.*

*Awake, arise, behold thou hast*
*Thy Life a Leaf, thy Breath a Blast;*
*At Night lye down prepar'd to have*
*Thy sleep, thy death, thy bed, thy grave.*

Learn these four Lines by Heart.

*Have Communion with few.*
*Be Intimate with ONE.*
*Deal justly with all.*
*Speak Evil of none.*

The Names and Order of the Books
of the Old and New-Testament.

| | |
|---|---|
| **G**Enesis | Levitieus |
| Exodus | Numbers |

| | |
|---|---|
| Deuteronomy | Iſaiah |
| Joſhua | Jeremiah |
| Judges | Lamentations |
| Ruth | Ezekiel |
| I. Samuel | Daniel |
| II. Samuel | Hoſea |
| I. Kings | Joel |
| II. Kings | Amos |
| I. Chronicles | Obadiah |
| II. Chronicles | Jonah |
| Ezra | Micah |
| Nehemiah | Nahum |
| Eſther | Habakkuk |
| Job | Zephaniah |
| Pſalms | Haggai |
| Proverbs | Zechariah |
| Eccleſiaſtes | Malachi. |
| Solomons Song | |

Matthew

| | |
|---|---|
| Matthew | I Timothy. |
| Mark | II. Timothy |
| Luke | Titus |
| John | Philemon |
| The Acts | Hebrews |
| Romans | James |
| I. Corinthians | I. Peter |
| II. Corinthians | II. Peter |
| Galatians | I. John |
| Ephesians | II. John |
| Philippians | III. John |
| Colossians | Jude |
| I. Thessalonians | Revelations |
| II. Thessalonians | |

*The numeral Letters and Figures, which serve for the ready finding of any Chapter, Psalm, and Verse in the Bible.*

| | | |
|---|---|---|
| i. | I | one |
| ii | 2 | two |
| iii | 3 | three |

| | | |
|---|---|---|
| iv | 4 | four |
| v | 5 | five |
| vi | 6 | six |
| vii | 7 | seven |
| viii | 8 | eight |
| ix | 9 | nine |
| x | 10 | ten |
| xi | 11 | eleven |
| xii | 12 | twelve |
| xiii | 13 | thirteen |
| xiv | 14 | fourteen |
| xv | 15 | fifteen |
| xvi | 16 | sixteen |
| xvii | 17 | seventeen |
| xviii | 18 | eighteen |
| xix | 19 | nineteen |
| xx | 20 | twenty |
| xxi | 21 | twenty one |
| xxii | 22 | twenty two |
| xxiii | 23 | twenty three |
| xxiv | 24 | twenty four |
| xxv | 25 | twenty five |
| xxvi | 26 | twenty six |
| xxvii | 27 | twenty seven |
| xxviii | 28 | twenty eight |

| | | |
|---|---|---|
| xxix | 29 | twenty nine |
| xxx | 30 | thirty |
| xxxi | 31 | thirty one |
| xxxii | 32 | thirty two |
| xxxiii | 33 | thirty three |
| xxxiv | 34 | thirty four |
| xxxv | 35 | thirty five |
| xxxvi | 36 | thirty six |
| xxxvii | 37 | thirty seven |
| xxxviii | 38 | thirty eight |
| xxxix | 39 | thirty nine |
| xl | 40 | forty |
| xli | 41 | forty one |
| xlii | 42 | forty two |
| xliii | 43 | forty three |
| xliv | 44 | forty four |
| xlv | 45 | forty five |
| xlvi | 46 | forty six |
| xlvii | 47 | forty seven |
| xlviii | 48 | forty eight |
| xlix | 49 | forty nine |
| l | 50 | fifty |
| li | 51 | fifty one |
| lii | 52 | fifty two |
| liii | 53 | fifty three |

| | | |
|---|---|---|
| liv | 54 | fifty four |
| lv | 55 | fifty five |
| lvi | 56 | fifty fix |
| lvii | 57 | fifty feven |
| lviii | 58 | fifty eight |
| lix | 59 | fifty nine |
| lx | 60 | fixty |
| lxi | 61 | fixty one |
| lxii | 62 | fixty two |
| lxiii | 63 | fixty three |
| lxiv | 64 | fixty four |
| lxv | 65 | fixty five |
| lxvi | 66 | fixty fix |
| lxvii | 67 | fixty feven |
| lxviii | 68 | fixty eight |
| lxix | 69 | fixty nine |
| lxx | 70 | feventy |
| lxxi | 71 | feventy one |
| lxxii | 72 | feventy two |
| lxxiii | 73 | feventy three |
| lxxiv | 74 | feventy four |
| lxxv | 75 | feventy five |
| lxxvi | 76 | feventy fix |
| lxxvii | 77 | feventy feven |
| lxxviii | 78 | feventy eight |

| | | |
|---|---|---|
| lxxix | 79 | feventy nine |
| lxxx | 80 | eighty |
| lxxxj | 81 | eighty one |
| lxxxii | 82 | eighty two |
| lxxxiii | 83 | eighty three |
| lxxxiv | 84 | eighty four |
| lxxxv | 85 | eighty five |
| lxxxvi | 86 | eighty fix |
| lxxxvii | 87 | eighty feven |
| lxxxviii | 88 | eighty eight |
| lxxxix | 89 | eighty nine |
| xc | 90 | ninety |
| xcj | 91 | ninety one |
| xcii | 92 | ninety two |
| xciii | 93 | ninety three |
| xciv | 94 | ninety four |
| xcv | 95 | ninety five |
| xcvi | 96 | ninety fix |
| xcvii | 97 | ninety feven |
| xcviii | 93 | ninety eight |
| xcix | 99 | ninety nine |
| c | 100 | an hundred |

# Mr.

MR. *John Rogers*, Minister of the Gospel in *London*, was the firstMartyr in Q. *Mary's*Reign, and was burnt at*Smithfield*,*February* the fourteenth, 1554. His Wife, with nine smallChildren, and one at at her Breast, following him to the Stake, with which sorrowful sight he was not in the least daunted, but with wonderful Patience died couragiously for the Gospel of Jesus Christ.

*Some few Days before his Death, he writ the following Exhortation to his Children.*

Give ear my Children to my words,
  whom God hath dearly bought,
Lay up his Laws within your heart,
  and print them in your thought,
I leave you here a little Book,
  for you to look upon:
That you may see your Fathers face,
  when he is dead and gone.
Who for the hope of heavenly things,
  while he did here remain,
Gave over all his golden Years
  to Prison and to Pain.
Where I among my Iron Bands,
  inclosed in the dark,

C

Not many days before my Death.
I did compose this Work.
And for Example to your Youth,
to whom I wish all good ;
I send you here God's perfect Truth,
and seel it with my Blood
To you my Heirs of earthly Things;
which I do leave behind,
That you may read and understand,
and keep it in your mind.
That as you have been Heirs of thet
which once shall wear away,
You also may possess that part,
which never shall decay.
Keep always GOD before your eyery
with all your whole intent ;
Commit no Sin in any wise,
keep his Commandement.
Abhor that arrant Whore of Rome,
and all her Blasphemies ;
And drink not of her cursed Cup,
obey not her decrees.
Give honour to your Mother dear,
remember well her pain ;

And recompenſe her in her Age
  with the like love again.
Be always ready for her help,
  and let her not decay;
Remember well your Father all .
  that ſhould have been your ſlay.
Give of your Portion to the Poor,
  as Riches do ariſe;
And from the needy naked Soul
  turn not away your eyes.
For he that doth not hear the cry
  of thoſe that ſtand in need,
Shall cry himſelf and not be heard,
  when he does hope to ſpeed.
If GOD hath given you increaſe
  and bleſſed well your ſtore,
Remember you are put in truſt,
  and ſhould relieve the poor.
Beware of feul and filthy Luſts,
  let ſuch things have no place,
Keep clean your Veſſels in the Lord,
  that he may you embrace.
Ye are the Temples of the Lord,
  for you are dearly bougbt .

And they that do defile the fame
    shall furely come to nought.
Be never Proud by any means,
    build not thy houfe too high,
But always have before yeur eyes,
    that you are born to die.
Defraud not him that hired is,
    your labour to fuftain;
And pay him ftill without delay,
    his wages for bis pain.
And as you would another Man
    againft you fhould proceed,
Do you the fame to them again,
    if they do ftand in need.
Impart your Fortion to the Poor,
    in Money and in Meat,
And fend the feeble fainting Soul
    of that which you do eat.
Ask Counfel always of the wife,
    give ear unto the end,
And ne'r refufe the fweet rebuke
    of him that is thy Friend.
Be always thankful to the Lord,
    with Prayer and with Praife,

Begging of him to blefs your work,
    and to direct your ways.
Seek firft I fay the living GOD,
    and always him adore;
And then be fure that he will blefs
    your basket and your ftore.
And I befeech Almighty GOD,
    replenifh you with Grace,
That I may meet you in the Heav'ns,
    and fee you face to face.
And tho' the Fire my Body burns,
    contrary to my kind;
That I cannot enjoy your love,
    according to my mind.
Yet I do bope that when the Heav'ns,
    fhall vanifh like a fcrowl,
I fhall fee you in perfect fhape,
    in Body and in Soul,
And that I may enjoy your love,
    and you enjoy the Land
I do befeech the living LORD
    to hold you in his hand.
Though here my Body be adjudg'd
    in flaming Fire to fry,

My Soul I truſt will ſtraight aſcend,
   to live with GOD on high.
What though this Carcaſe ſmart a while,
   what though this Life decay,
My Soul I truſt will be with GOD,
   and live with him for aye.
I know I am a Sinner born,
   from the Original;
And that I do deſerve to die,
   by my Fore-Fathers fall.
But by our Saviour's precious Blood,
   which on the Croſs was ſpilt,
Who freely offer'd up his Life,
   to ſave our Souls from Guilt,
I hope Redemption I ſhall have,
   and all that in him truſt;
When I ſhall ſee him face to face,
   and live among the Juſt.
Why then ſhould I fear Deaths grim look,
   ſince Chriſt for me did die?
For King and Cæſar, Rich and Poor,
   the force of Death, muſt trie.
When I am chained to the Stake,
   and Faggots girt me round,

Then pray the Lord my Soul in Heav'n
   may be with Glory crown'd.
Come welcome Death, the end of fears,
   I am prepar'd to die;
Those earthly Flames will send my Soul,
   up to the Lord on high.
Farewel my Children to the World,
   where you must yet remain,
The Lord of Host be your defence
   till we do meet again.
Farewel my true and loving Wife,
   my Children and my Friends,
I hope in Heaven to see you all,
   when all things have their ends
If you go on to serve the Lord,
   as you have now begun,
You shall walk safely all your days,
   until your life be done.
GOD grant you so to end your days,
   as he shall think it best,
That I may meet you in the Heav'ns,
   where I do hope to rest.

The

# The SHORTER
# CATECHISM

Agreed upon by the Reverend

*Assembly of* Divines *at Westminster*

Quest *W*Hat is the chief End
of Man ?
*Answ.* Man's chief End is to
Glorify God, and to Enjoy Him
for ever.

Q. *What Rule hath God given to
direct us how we may glorify and
enjoy Him ?*
A. The Word of God which is
contained in the Scriptures of the
Old

Old and New Teſtament, is th
only Rule to direct us how we
may glorify and enjoy him.

Q. *What do the Scriptures prin-*
*cipally teach ?*

A. The Scriptures principally
teach, what Man is to believe concerning God, and what duty God
requireth of Man.

Q. *What is God ?*

A. God is a Spirit, Infinite, E-
ternal, and Unchangeable, in His
Being, Wiſdom, Power, Holineſs,
Juſtice, Goodneſs and Truth.

Q. *Are there more Gods than One ?*

A. There is but ONE only,
the living and true God.

Q. *How many Perſons are there*
*in the God-head ?*

A. There are Three Perſons in

the God-Head, the Father, the Son, and the Holy Ghoſt, & theſe Three are One GOD the ſame in Subſtance, equal in Power & Glory.

Q. What are the Decrees of God?

A. The Decrees of God are his eternal Purpoſe, according to the Counſel of his own Will, whereby for his own Glory, he hath fore-ordained whatſoever comes to paſs

Q. How doth God execute his Decrees?

A. God executeth his Decrees in the Works of Creation & Providence.

Q. What is the Work of Creation?

A. The Work of Creation is God's Making all things of Nothing, by the Word of his Power,

in

in the space of six days, & all ve
ry good.

Q. *How did God create Man ?*

A. God created Man Male and
Female, after his own Image, in
Knowledge, Righteousness, and
Holiness, 'with Dominion over
the Creatures

Q *What are Gods Works of Providence?*

A. God's Works of Providence
are his most holy, wise & power-
ful preserving & govering all his
Creatures and all their Actions.

Q *What special Act of Providence
did God exercise towards Man in the
Estate wherein he was created ?*

A. When God had created Man,
He entred into a Covenant of Life
with him, upon condition of perfect
Obedience, forbidding him to Eat

of the Tree of knowledge of good and evil upon pain of Death.

*Q. Did our first Parents continue in the estate wherein they were created?*

A. Our first Parents being left to the freedom of their own Will, fell from the estate wherein they were created, by sinning against God.

*Q. What is Sin !*

A. Sin is any want of Conformity unto, or Transgression of the Law of God.

*Q. What was the Sin whereby our first Parents fell from the estate wherein they were created?*

A. The Sin whereby our first Parents fell from the estate wherein they were created, was their eating the forbidden fruit.

Q. Did

Q. *Did all Mankind fall in* A-dam's *firſt tranſgreſſion* ?

A. The Covenant being made with *Adam*, not only for himſelf but for his Poſterity, all Mankind deſcending from him by ordinary Generation, ſinned in him, & fell with him in his firſt tranſgreſſion.

Q. *Into what eſtate did the Fall bring Mankind* ?

A. The Fall brought Mankind into an eſtate of Sin and Miſery.

Q. *Wherein conſiſts the ſinfulneſs of that eſtate whereinto Man fell* ?

A. The ſinfulneſs of that eſtate whereintoMan fell, conſiſts in the Guilt of *Adam*'s firſt Sin, the want of OriginalRighteouſneſs, and the Corruption of his whole Nature, which is commonlycalledOriginal

Sin, together withall actual Transgressions which proceed from it.

Q. *What is the Misery of that estate whereinto Man fell?*

A. All Mankind by their fall, lost Communion with God, are under his Wrath & Curse, and so made liable to all Miseries in this Life, to Death it self, and to the pains of Hell for ever.

Q. *Did God leave all Mankind to perish in the estate of Sin & Misery?*

A. God having out of his meer good pleasure from all Eternity, Elected some to everlasting Life, did enter into a Covenant of Grace, to deliver them out of the state of Sin & Misery, and to being them into a state of Salvation by a Redeemer,                Q. *Who*

Q Who is the Redeemer of Gods El.

A. The only Redeemer of God a Elect, is the Lord Jesus Chrift, who being the eternal Son of God, became Man, and fo was, and continues to be God and Man in two diftinct Natures, and one Perfon for ever.

Q. How did Chrift being the Son of God become Man ?

A. Chrift the Son of God became Man, by taking to himfelf a true Body and a reafonable Soul, being conceived by the power of the Holy Ghoft, in the Womb of the Virgin Mary, and born of her, and yet without Sin.

Q. What Offices doth Chrift execute as our Redeemer ?

A. Chrift

A. Chrift as our Redeemer executes theOffice of a Prophet, of a Prieft, and of a King, both in his eftate ofHumſliation&Exaltation.

Q. *How doth Chrift execute the Office of a Prophet ?*

A.Chrift executeth theOffice of a Prophet, in revealing to us by his Word and Spirit, the Will of God for our Salvation.

Q. *How doth Chrift execute the Office of a Prieft-*

A Chrift executeth the Office of a Prieft, in his once offering up himſelf a Sacrifice toſatisfy Divine Juftice, & reconcile us toGod, & in makingcontinual Interceffionfor us

Q *How doth Chrift execute the Office of a King ?*

A. Chrift executeth theOffice of

a King, in subduing us to himself in ruling and defending us, and in restraining and conquering all his and our Enemies.

Q. *Wherein did Chriſt's Humiliation conſiſt?*

A. Chriſt'sHumiliation conſiſted in His being born, and that in a low condition, madeunder thelaw undergoing the miſeries ofthis *life* the wrath of God, and the curſed Death of the Croſs, in being buried and continuing under the power of Death for a time.

Q*Wherein conſiſtsChriſts Exaltation*

A. Chriſt's Exaltation conſiſteth in his riſing again from theDead on the third day, in aſcending up into Heaven, &ſitting at theRight

D      Hand

Hand of God the Father, and in coming to judge the World at the laſt Day.

Q. *How are we made Partakers of the Redemption purchaſed by Chriſt?*

A. We are made Partakers of the Redemption purchaſed by Chriſt, by the effectual Application of it to us by his Holy Spirit.

Q. *How doth the Spirit apply to us the Redemption purchaſed by Chriſt?*

A. The Spirit applieth to us the Redemption purchaſed by Chriſt, by working Faith in us, & thereby uniting us to Chriſt in our effectual Calling.

Q. *What is effectual Calling?*

A. Effectual Calling is the Work of God's Spirit, whereby convincing us of our Sin & Miſery, en-

lightning ourMinds in theKnow-
ledge of Chrilt, & renewing our
Wills,he doth perfwade &enable
us to embrace Jefus Chrilt, freely offered to us in theGofpel.

*Q What Benefits do they that are effec-
tually called partake of in this Life?*

A. They that areEffectually called,do in thisLife partake of Juftification, Adoption, Sanctification, & the feveral Benefits which
in this Life do either accompany
or flow from them.

Q What is *Juftification* ?

A. Juftification is an act of God's
freeGrace,wherein he pardoneth
all our Sins, and accepteth us as
righteous in his fight,only for the
righteoufnefs ofChrilt imputed to
us, and received by Faith alone,

Q. *What is Adoption ?*

A. Adoption is an Act of God's FreeGrace, whereby we are received into the Number, and have Right to all the Priviledges of the Sons of God

Q. *What is Sanctification ?*

A. Sanctification is the Work of God's freeGrace, whereby we are renewed in the whole Man, after the Image of God, & are enabled more & more to die unto Sin, & live unto Righteousness.

Q. *What are the Benefits which in this life do accompany or fl. w from Justification, Adoption & Sanctification ?*

A. The Benefits which in this Life do accompany or flow from Justification, Adoption or Sanctification, are assurance of God's love, peace of Conscience, joy in the Holy Ghost, increase of Grace, & perseverance therein to the end.

Q. *What benefits do Believers receive from Christ at their Death?*

A. The Souls of Believers are at their Death made perfect in Holiness, & do immediately pass into Glory, & their Bodies being still united to Christ, do rest in their Graves till the Resurrection.

Q. *What benefits do Believers receive from Christ at the Resurrection?*

A. At the Resurrection Believers being raised up to Glory, shall be openly acknowledged & acquitted in the Day of Judgment, & made perfectly blessed in full enjoying of God, to all Eternity.

Q. *What is the Duty which God*

*requires of Man ?*

*A.* The Duty which God requires of Man, is Obedience to his revealed will.

*Q. What did God at first reveal to Man for the Rule of his Obedience ?*

*A.* The Rule which God at first revealed to Man for his Obedience was the Moral Law.

*Q. Where is the Moral Law summarily comprehended ?*

*A.* The Moral Law is summarily comprehended in the Ten Commandments.

*Q. What is the Sum of the Ten Commandments ?*

*A.* The Sum of the Ten Commandments is, To love the Lord our God with all our Heart, with all our Souls, and with all our

Strength, and with all our Mind, and our Neighbour as ourselves.

Q. *What is the Preface to the Ten Commandments?*

A. The Preface to the Ten Commandments is in these Words, *I am the Lord thy God, which have brought thee out of the Land of Egypt, out of the House of Bondage.*

Q. *What doth the Preface to the Ten Commandments teach us?*

A. The Preface to the Ten Commandments teacheth us, that because God is the Lord, & our God and Redeemer, therefore we are bound to keep all his Commandments.

Q. *Which is the first Commandment?*

A. The first Commandment is, *Thou shalt have no other gods before Me.*

Q. *What is required in the first Commandment?*

A. The first Commandment requireth us to know and acknowledge God to be the only true God and our God, and to worship and glorify him accordingly.

Q. *What is forbidden in the first Commandment?*

A. The first Commandment forbiddeth the denying, or not worshipping and glorifying the true God, as God and our God, & the giving that Worship and Glory to any other which is due to him alone

Q. *What are the specially taught by these Words* (Before Me)*in the first Commandment?*

A. These Words (*Before me*) in the first Commandment, teach us,

ThatGod who seeth all things, taketh notice of, and is much displeased with the Sin of having any other god.

Q *Which is the second Commandment?*

*A.* The second Commandment is, *Thou shalt not make unto thee any Graven Image, or any likeness of any thing that is in Heaven above, or that is in the Earth beneath, or that is in the Water under the Earth: Thou shalt not bow down thy self to them, nor serve them, for I the Lord thy God am a jealous God, visiting the Iniquities of the Fathers upon the Children, unto the third and fourth Generation of them that hate me, & shewing mercy unto thousands of them that love me, and keep my Commandments.*

Q. *What is required in the second*

*Commandment ?*

*A.* The second Commandment requireth the receiving, observing, & keeping pure & entire all such religious Worship & Ordinances, as God hath appointed in his Word

*Q. What is forbidden in the second Commandment ?*

*A.* The second Commandment forbiddeth the worshipping of God by Images, or any other way, nor appointed in his Word.

*Q. What are the Reasons annexed to the second Commandment ?*

*A.* The Reasons annexed to the second Commandment, are God's Sovereignty over us, his Propriety in us, and the Zeal he hath to his own Worship.

*Q Which is the third Commandment?*

*A.* The third Commandment is, *Thou shalt not take the Name of the Lord thy God in vain; for the Lord will not hold him guiltless that taketh his Name in vain.*

*Q. What is required in the third Commandment?*

*A.* The third Commandment requireth the holy & reverend use of God's Name, Titles, Attributes, Ordinances, Word and Works.

*Q. What is forbidden in the third Commandment?*

*A.* The third Commandment forbiddeth all prophaning or abusing of any thing whereby God maketh himself known.

*Q What is the Reason annexed to the third Commandment?*

*A.* The Reason annexed to the

Third Commandment is, That however the Breakers of this Commandment may escape Punishment from Men yet the Lord our God will not suffer them to escape his righteous Judgment.

*Q. Which is the fourth Commandment?*

*A.* The fourth Commandment is, *Remember the Sabbath-Day to keep it Holy six Days shalt thou labour & do all thy Work, but the seventh Day is the Sabbath of the Lord thy God, in it thou shalt not do any work; thou nor thy Son, nor thy Daughter, thy Manservant, nor thy Maid servant, nor thy Cattle, nor the Stranger that is within thy Gates ; for in six Days the Lord made Heaven & Earth, the Sea, and all that in them is, & rested the seventh Day, wherefore the Lord blessed the* Sabbath Day, *and hallowed it.*

*Q. What is required in the fourth Commandment ?*

A. The fourth Commandment requireth the keeping holy to God ſuch ſet times as he hath appointed in his Word, expreſly one whole Day in ſeven to be an holy Sabbath to Himſelf.

*Q Which day of the ſeven hath God appointed to be the weekly Sabbath ?*

A. From the beginning of the World to the Reſurrection of *Chriſt* God appointed the ſeventh Day of the Week to be the weekly Sabbath, and the firſt Day of the Week ever ſince, to continue to the end of the World, which is the Chriſtian Sabbath.

*Q. How is the Sabbath to be ſanctified ?*

*A.* The Sabbath is to be fanctified by an holy refting all that Day, even from fuch worldly Employments & Recreations, as are lawful on other Days, & fpending the whole time in publick & private exercifes of God's Worfhip, except fo much as is to be taken up in the Works of Neceffity & Mercy.

*Q What is forbidden in the fourth Commandment ?*

*A.* The fourth Commandment forbiddeth the Omiffion or carelefs Performance of the Duties required, & the prophaning the Day by idlenefs, or doing that which is in it felf finful, or by unneceffary Thoughts, Words or Works, about worldly Employments or Recreations.

Q. *What are the Reasons annex-ed to the fourth Commandment ?*

A. The Reasons annexed to the fourth Commandment, are God's allowing us six Days of the Week for our own Employments, His challenging a special Propriety in the seventh, his own Example, and his blessing the Sabbath Day.

Q. *Which is the fifth Commandment ?*

A. The fifth Commandment is, *Honour thy Father & thy Mother, that thy Days may be long upon the land which the Lord thy God giveth that.*

Q. *What is required in the fifth Commandment ?*

A. The fifth Commandment requireth the preserving the Honour & performing the Duties belong ing to every one in their several

Places and Relations, as Superiours, Inferiours, or Equals.

Q *What is forbidden in the fifth Commandment?*

A. The fifth Commandment forbiddeth the neglecting or doing any thing against the Honour and Duty which belongeth to every one in their several Places & Relations.

Q. *What is the Reason annexed to the fifth Commandment?*

A. The Reason annexed to the fifth Commandment, is a promise of long Life & Prosperity, (as far as it shall serve for God's Glory and their own good) to all such as keep this Commandment.

Q. *Which is the sixth Commandment?*

A. The sixth Commandment is,

*Thou shalt not Kill.*

Q. *What is required in the sixth* Commandment ?

A. The sixth Commandment requireth all lawful Endeavours to preserve our own Life, and the Life of others.

Q. *What is forbidden in the sixth* Commandment ?

A. The sixth Commandment forbiddeth the taking away of our own Life, or the Life of our Neighbour unjustly, and whatsoever tendeth thereunto.

Q *Which is the seventh Commandment*

A. The seventh Commandment is, *Thou shalt not commit Adultery.*

Q. *What is required in the se-* *venth Commandment ?*

E                    A

*A.* The seventh Commandment requireth the preservation of our own, and our Neighbour's Chastity, in Heart, Speech & Behaviour.

*Q. What is forbidden in the seventh Commandment ?*

*A.* The seventh Commandment forbiddeth all unchast Thoughts, Words and Actions.

*Q Which is the eighth Commandment?*

*A.* The eighth Commandment is, *Thou shalt not Steal.*

*Q What is required in the eighth Commandment ?*

*A.* The eighth Commandment requireth the lawful procuring & furthering the Wealth & outward Estate of our selves and others.

*Q. What is forbidden in the eighth Commandment ?*

*A.* The eighth Commandment forbiddeth whatfoever doth, or may unjuftly hinder our own, or our Neighbours Wealth or outward Eftate.

*Q. Which is the ninth Commandment*

*A.* The ninth Commandment is, *Thou shalt not bear false Witness against thy Neighbour.*

*Q. What is required in the ninth Commandment?*

*A.* The ninth Commandment requireth the maintaining and promoting of Truth between Man and Man, and of our own, & our Neighbours good Name, especially in Witnefs bearing.

*Q What is forbidden in the ninth Commandment?*

*A.* The ninth Commandment forbiddeth whatsoever is prejudicial to Truth, or injurious to our own or our Neighbours good Name.

Q Which is the Tenth Commandment?

A. The Tenth Commandment is, *Thou shalt not covet thy Neighbour's House, thou shalt not covet thy Neighbour's Wife, nor his Man servant, nor his Maid servant, nor his Ox, nor his Ass, nor any thing that is thy Neighbours.*

Q. *What is required in the tenth Commandment ?*

A. The tenth Commandment requireth full Contentment with our own Condition, with a right & charitable frame of Spirit towards our Neighbour, & all that is his.

Q *What is forbidden in the tenth Commandment ?*

*A.* The Tenth Commandment forbiddeth all Discontentment with our own estate, envying or grieving at the good of our Neighbour, and all inordinate motions & affections to any thing that is his.

*Q Is any Man able perfectly to keep the Commandments of God ?*

*A.* No meer man since the Fall is able in this Life perfectly to keep the Commandments of God, but daily doth break them in Thought, Word and Deed.

*Q Are all Transgressions of the Law equally heinous ?*

*A.* Some Sins in themselves, & by reason of several Aggravations are more heinous in the sight of God than others.

*Q What doth every sin deserve ?*

*A.* Every Sin deserveth God's Wrath and Curse, both in this Life, and that which is to come.

*Q. What doth God require of us, that we may escape his Wrath and Curse, due unto us for Sin?*

*A,* To escape the Wrath & Curse of God due to us for Sin, God requireth of us Faith in Jesus Christ, Repentance unto Life, with the diligent use of all outward Means whereby Christ communicateth to us the benefits of Redemption,

*Q. What is Faith in Jesus Christ?*

*A.* Faith in Jesus Christ is a saving Grace, whereby we receive and rest upon him alone for Salvation, as He is offered to us in the Gospel

*Q. What is Repentance unto Life?*

*A.* Repentance unto Life, is a faving Grace, whereby a Sinner out of a true fenfe of his Sin, and apprehenfion of the Mercy of God in Chrift, doth with grief & hatred of his Sin, turn from it unto God, with full purpofe of, & endeavour after new Ohedience.

*Q. What are the outward & ordinary means whereby Chrift communion-telb to us the benefits of Redemption?*

*A.* The outward and ordinary means whereby Chrift communicareth to us the benefits of Redemption are his Ordinances, efpecially the Word, Sacraments & Prayer; all which are made effectual to the Elect for Salvation.

*Q. How is the word made effectual to Salvation?*

*A.* The Spirit of God maketh the Reading, but especially the Preaching of the Word an effectual Means of Convincing & Converting Sinners, and of building them up in Holiness & Comfort, through Faith unto Salvation.

*Q. How is the Word to be Read and Heard that it may become effectual to Salvation ?*

That the Word may become effectual to Salvation, we must attend thereunto with diligence, Preparation & Prayer, receive it with Faith & Love, lay it up in our Hearts, & practice it in our Lives.

*Q. How doth the Sacraments become effectual means of Salvation?*

*A.* The Sacraments become effectual Means of Salvation, not

from any vertue in them, or in him
that doth administer them, but
only by the blessing of Christ, and
the working of the Spirit in them
that by Faith receive them.

Q. *What is a Sacrament?*

A. A Sacrament is an holy Or-
dinance instituted by Christ,
wherein by sensible Signs, Christ
and the benefits of the New Covenant are represented, sealed, and
applied to Believers.

Q. *Which are the Sacraments of
the New Testament?*

A. The Sacraments of the New
Testament, are Baptism, and the
Lord's Supper.

Q. *What is Baptism?*

A. Baptism is a Sacrament, wherein by washing with Water in the

Name of the Father, & of the Son, and of the Holy Ghost, doth signify and seal our ingrafting into Christ, & partaking of the benefits of the Covenant of Grace, and our Engagement to be the Lord's.

Q. *To whom is Baptism to be administred?*

A Baptism is not to be administred to any that are out of the visible Church, till they profess their Faith in Christ, and Obedience to Him, but the Infants of such as are Members of the visible Church are to be Baptised.

Q. *What is the Lord's Supper?*

A. The Lord's Supper is a Sacrament, wherein by giving and receiving Bread & Wine according to Christ Appointment, His

Death is ſhewed forth, and the worthy Receivers are not after a corporal and carnal Manner, but by Faith made Partakers of His Body & Blood, with all his bene-fits, to their Spiritual Nouriſh-ment and growth in Grace.

Q. *What is required in the wor-thy receiving of the Lord's Supper?*

A. It is required of them that would worthily partake of the Lold'sSupper, that they examine themſelvesoftheirKnowledge to diſcern the Lord'sBody, of their Faith to feed upon Him, of their Repentance, Love, & new Obedi-ence, leſtcomingunworthily, they eat and drink judgment to them-ſelves.

Q. *What is Prayer ?*.

*A* Prayer is an offering up of our Defires to God, for Things a-greeable to His Will, in the Name of Chrift, with Confeffion of our Sins, and thankful Acknowledgment of his Meicies.

Q. *What Rule hath God given for our Direction in Prayer?*

*A* The whole Word of God is of ufe to direct us in Prayer, but the fpecial Rule of Direction is that form of Prayer which Chrift taught His Difciples, commonly called, *The Lord's Prayer.*

Q. *What doth the Preface of the Lord's Prayer teach us?*

*A.* The Preface of the Lord's Prayer, which is, *Our Father which art in Heaven,* teacheth us to draw near to God with all holy Reve-

rence, and Confidence, as Chi
to a Father, able & ready to
us, and that we should pray
and for others.

*Q What do we pray for in the first Peti*

*A.* In the first Petition, which
*Hallowed be thy Name*, we pr
that God would enable us and
thers, to glorify Him in all t
whereby he makes himself kn
and that He would dispose
things to His own Glory.

*Q What do we pray for in the 2nd Petit*

*A.* In the second Petition, which
is, *Thy Kingdom come*, we pray that
Satan's Kingdom may be destroy-
ed, the Kingdom of Grace may be
advanced, ourselves & others *bro't*
into it, & kept in it, & that the
Kingdom of Glory may be hastned.

*What do we pray for in the Petition ?*

In the third Petition, which *by Will be done on Earth as it is eaven,* we pray, that God by Grace, would make us able & ling to know, obey & submit his Will in all things, as the els do in Heaven.

*at do we pray for in the 4th Petition*

a the fourth Petition, which *ve us this Day our daily Bread,* pray, that of God s free Gift we may receive a competent Portion of the good things of this Life, and enjoy his blessing with them.

Q *What do we pray for in the 5th Petition*

A. In the fifth Petition, which is, *And forgive us our Debts, as we forgive our Debtors,* we pray, that

God, for Chrift's fake, would freely pardon all our fins, which we are rather encouraged to afk, becaufe by his grace we are enabled from the heart to forgive others.

Q. *What do we pray for in the .1th petition?*

A. In the fixth petition, which is, *And lead us not into temptation, but deliver us from evil,* we pray, that God would either keep us from being tempted to fin, or fupport and deliver us when we are tempted.

Q. *What doth the conclusion of the Lord's prayer teach us?*

A. The conclufion of the Lord's prayer, which is, *For thine is the kingdom, and the power, and the glory forever, Amen,* teacheth us to make our encouragement in prayer from God only, and in our prayers to

[*Restoration of lacking text*]

praife him, afcribing kingdom, power and glory to him, and in tefti-
mony of our defires, and afsurance
to be heard, we fay, Amen.

*[ Restoration of lacking text]*

78